"We'll Get Engaged."

"Engaged?" Her eyes went wild and she jerked away from the brush of his arm as if scorched. "You've got to be kidding. Don't you think getting married to pacify the press is a little extreme?"

"It won't go that far. Once the buzz dies down and they focus on the issues again, you and I will quietly break up."

Yeah, the idea of lying chaffed more than a little since he considered his ethics to be of the utmost importance. But right now, only one thing dominated his thoughts.

Keeping Ashley's reputation from suffering for his mistake.

She crossed her arms over her chest, her brown eyes glinting nearly black with determination that warned him he may have underestimated the strength of the woman beside him.

"You are out of your flipping mind. There's not a chance in hell you're putting an engagement ring on my finger."

Dear Reader,

Welcome to the first book in my new LANDIS BROTHERS series! Thank you so much to those of you who asked to see more of these hunky heroes-to-be after reading about them in my Silhouette Romantic Suspense *Holiday Heroes*. And thanks as well for all the awesome notes requesting Ashley Carson's story after reading my first two Silhouette Desires about her foster sisters. It's a delight to pair Ashley with the oldest Landis brother.

On a personal note, I especially enjoy the opportunity to set these stories in South Carolina where I grew up. Furthermore, while my sisters and I were at the College of Charleston, we all met our future husbands, cadets at The Citadel. Charleston will always be the city of romance to me. I hope you find the area as enchanting as I still do!

I very much enjoy hearing from readers. If you would like to contact me, I can be reached at P.O. Box 6065, Navarre, FL 32566 or www.catherinemann.com.

Happy Reading!

Catherine Mann

CATHERINE MANN

RICH MAN'S FAKE FIANCÉE

Published by Silhouette Books

America's Publisher of Contemporary Romance

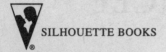

SILHOUETTE BOOKS

ISBN-13: 978-0-373-76878-3
ISBN-10:   0-373-76878-8

RICH MAN'S FAKE FIANCÉE

Copyright © 2008 by Catherine Mann

All rights reserved. Except for use in any review, the reproduction or utilization of this work in whole or in part in any form by any electronic, mechanical or other means, now known or hereafter invented, including xerography, photocopying and recording, or in any information storage or retrieval system, is forbidden without the written permission of the editorial office, Silhouette Books, 233 Broadway, New York, NY 10279 U.S.A.

This is a work of fiction. Names, characters, places and incidents are either the product of the author's imagination or are used fictitiously, and any resemblance to actual persons, living or dead, business establishments, events or locales is entirely coincidental.

This edition published by arrangement with Harlequin Books S.A.

® and TM are trademarks of Harlequin Books S.A., used under license. Trademarks indicated with ® are registered in the United States Patent and Trademark Office, the Canadian Trade Marks Office and in other countries.

Visit Silhouette Books at www.eHarlequin.com

Printed in U.S.A.

CATHERINE MANN

RITA® Award winner Catherine Mann resides on a sunny Florida beach with her military flyboy husband and their four children. Although after nine moves in twenty years, she hasn't given away her winter gear! With more than a million books in print in fifteen countries, she has also celebrated five RITA® finals, three Maggie Award of Excellence finals and a Booksellers' Best win. A former theater school director and university teacher, she graduated with a master's degree in theater from UNC-Greensboro and a bachelor's degree in fine arts from the College of Charleston. Catherine enjoys hearing from readers and chatting on her message board—thanks to the wonders of the wireless Internet that allows her to cyber-network with her laptop by the water! To learn more about her work, visit her Web site at www.CatherineMann.com.

To my sisters, Julie Morrison and Beth Reaves,
and to their South Carolina husbands,
Todd Morrison and Jerry Reaves. Much love to you all!

And a great big thanks to my editor Melissa Jeglinski
for giving me the opportunity
to tell the Landis Brothers' stories!

One

Only one thing sucked worse than wearing boring white cotton underwear on the night she finally landed in bed with her secret fantasy man.

Having him walk out on her before daylight.

Ashley Carson tensed under her down comforter. Through the veil of her eyelashes, she watched her new lover quietly zip his custom-fit pants. She'd taken a bold step—unusual for her—by falling into bed with Matthew Landis the night before. Her still-tingly sated body cheered the risk. Her good sense, however, told her she'd made a whopper mistake with none other than South Carolina's most high-profile senatorial candidate.

Moonlight streaked through the dormer window, glinting off his dark hair trimmed short but still mussed from her fingers. Broad shoulders showcased his beacon white shirt, crisp even though she'd stripped it from him just hours ago when their planning session for his fund-raiser dinner at her restaurant/home had taken an unexpected turn down the hall to her bedroom.

Matthew may have been dream material, but safely so since she'd always thought there wasn't a chance they could actually end up together. *She* preferred a sedentary, quiet life running her business, with simple pleasures she never took for granted after her foster child upbringing. *He* worked in the spotlight as a powerful member of the House of Representatives just as adept at negotiating high-profile legislation as swinging a hammer at a Habitat for Humanity site.

People gravitated to his natural charisma and sense of purpose.

Matthew reached for his suit jacket draped over the back of a corner chair. Would he say goodbye or simply walk away? She wanted to think he would speak to her, but couldn't bear to find out otherwise so she sat up, floral sheet clutched to her chest.

"That floorboard by the door creaks, Matthew. You might want to sidestep it or I'll hear you sneaking out."

He stopped, wide shoulders stiffening before he turned slowly. He hadn't shaved, his five-o'clock shadow having thickened into something much darker—just below the guilty glint in his jewel-green eyes that had helped win him a seat in the U.S. House of Representatives. Five months from now, come November, he could well be the handsome sexy-eyed *Senator* Landis if he won the seat to be vacated by his mother.

With one quick blink, Matthew masked the hint of emotion. "Excuse me? I haven't snuck anywhere since I was twelve, trying to steal my cousin's magazines from under his mattress." He stuffed his tie in his pocket. "I was getting dressed."

"Oh, my mistake." She slid from the bed, keeping the sheet tucked around her naked body. The room smelled of potpourri and musk, but she wouldn't let either distract her. "Since yesterday, you've developed a light step and a penchant for walking around in your socks."

Ashley nodded toward his Gucci loafers dangling from two fingers.

"You were sleeping soundly," he stated simply.

A lot of great sex tends to wear a woman out. Apparently she hadn't accomplished the same for him, not that she intended to voice her vulnerability to him. "How polite of you."

He dropped the shoes to the floor and toed them

on one after the other. Seeing his expensive loafers on her worn hardwood floors with a cotton rag rug, she couldn't miss the hints that this polished, soon-to-be senator wasn't at home in her world. Too bad those reminders didn't stop her from wanting to drag him back onto her bed.

"Ashley, last night was amazing—"

"Stop right there. I don't need platitudes or explanations. We're both single adults, not dating each other or anyone else." She snagged a terry-cloth robe off a brass hook by the bathroom door and ducked inside to swap the sheet for the robe. "We're not even really friends for that matter. More like business acquaintances who happened to indulge in a momentary attraction."

Okay, momentary for him maybe. But she'd been salivating over him during the few times they'd met to plan social functions at her Beachcombers Restaurant and Bar.

Ashley stepped back into the bedroom, tugging the robe tie tight around her waist.

"Right, we're on the same page then." He braced a hand on the doorframe, his gold cuff links glinting.

"You should get going if you plan to make it home in time to change."

He hesitated for three long thumps of her heart before pivoting away on his heel. Ashley followed him down the hall of her Southern antebellum home-turned-restaurant she ran with her two foster sisters. She'd recently taken up residence in the back room off her office, watching over the accounting books as well as the building since her recently married sisters had moved out.

Sure enough, more than one floorboard creaked under his confident strides as they made their way past the gift shop and into the lobby. She unlocked the towering front door, avoiding his eyes. "I'll send copies of the signed contract for the fund-raising dinner to your campaign manager."

The night before, Matthew had stayed late after the business dinner to pass along some last-minute paperwork. She never could have guessed how combustible a simple brush of their bodies against each other could become. Her fantasies about this man had always revolved around far more exotic scenarios.

But they were just that. Fantasies. As much as he tried to hide his emotions, she couldn't miss how fast he'd made tracks out of her room. She'd been rejected often enough as a kid by her parents and even classmates. These days, pride starched her spine far better than any back brace she'd been forced to wear to combat scoliosis.

Matthew flattened a palm to the mahogany door. "I will call you later."

Sure. Right. "No calls." She didn't even want the

possibility of waiting by the phone, or worse yet, succumbing to the humiliating urge to dial him up, only to get stuck in voicejail as she navigated his answering service. "Let's end this encounter on the same note it started. Business."

She extended her hand. He eyed her warily. She pasted her poise in place through pride alone. Matthew enfolded her hand in his, not shaking after all, rather holding as he leaned forward to press a kiss…

On her cheek.

Damn.

He slipped out into the muggy summer night. "It's still dark. You should go back to sleep."

Sleep? He had to be freaking kidding.

Thank goodness she had plenty to keep her busy now that Matthew had left, because she was fairly certain she wouldn't be sleeping again. She watched his brisk pace down the steps and into the shadowy parking lot, which held only his Lexus sedan and her tiny Kia Rio. What was she doing, staring after him? She shoved the door closed with a heavy click.

All her poise melted. She still had her pride but her ability to stand was sorely in question. Ashley sagged against the counter by the antique cash register in the foyer.

She couldn't even blame him. She'd been a willing participant all night long. They'd been in the kitchen where she'd planned to give him a taste of the dessert pastries her sister added to the menu for his fund-raiser. Standing near each other in the close confines of the open refrigerator, they had brushed against each other, once, twice.

His hand had slowly raised to thumb away cream filling at the corner of her mouth...

She'd forgotten all about her white cotton underwear until he'd peeled it from her body on the way back to her bedroom. Then she hadn't been able to think of much else for hours to come.

Her bruised emotions needed some serious indulging. She gazed into the gift shop, her eyes locking on a rack of vintage-style lingerie. She padded on bare feet straight toward the pale pink satin nightgown dangling on the end. Her fingers gravitated to the wide bands of peekaboo lace crisscrossing over the bodice, rimming the hem, outlining the V slit in the front of the 1920s-looking garment.

How she'd ached for whispery soft underthings during her childhood, but had always been forced to opt for the more practical cotton, a sturdier fabric not so easily snagged by her back brace. She didn't need the brace any longer. Just a slight lift to her left shoulder remained, only noticeable if someone knew to check. But while she'd ditched the brace once it finished the job, she still felt each striation on her heart.

Ashley snatched the hanger from the rack and

dashed past the shelved volumes of poetry, around a bubble bath display to the public powder room. Too bad she hadn't worn this yesterday. Her night with Matthew might not have ended any differently, but at least she would have had the satisfaction of stamping a helluva sexier imprint on his memory.

A quick shrug landed her robe on the floor around her feet.

Ashley avoided the mirror, a habit long ingrained. She focused instead on the nightgown's beauty. One bridal shower after another, she'd gifted her two foster sisters with the same style.

Satin slid along her skin like a cool shower over a body still flushed from the joys of heated sex with Matthew. She sunk onto the tapestry chaise, a French Restoration piece she'd bargained for at an estate auction. She lit the candle next to her to complete the sensory saturation. The flame flickered shadows across the faded wallpaper, wafting relaxing hints of lavender.

One deep breath at a time, she willed her anger to roll free as she drifted into the pillowy cloud of sensation. She tugged a decorative afghan over her. Maybe she could snag a nano nap after all.

Timeless relaxing moments later, Ashley inhaled again, deeper. And coughed. She sat up bolt right, sniffing not lavender, but…

Smoke.

* * *

Staring out at the summer sunrise just peeking up from the ocean, Matthew Landis worked like hell to get his head together before he powered back up those steps to retrieve the briefcase he'd left behind at Beachcombers.

He slid his car into Park for the second time that day, back where he'd started—with Ashley Carson. He prided himself on never making a misstep thanks to diligent planning. His impulsive tumble with her definitely hadn't been planned.

As a public servant he'd vowed to look out for the best interests of the people, protect and help others, especially the vulnerable. Yet last night he'd taken advantage of one of the most vulnerable women he knew.

He'd always been careful in choosing bed partners, because while he never intended to marry, he damn well couldn't live his life as a monk. He'd already had his one shot at forever in college, only to lose her to heart failure from a rare birth defect. He'd never even gotten the chance to introduce Dana to his family. No one knew about their engagement to this day. The notion of sharing that information with anyone had always felt like he would be giving up a part of their short time together.

After that, he'd focused on finishing his MBA at Duke University and entering the family business of politics. His inheritance afforded him the option of serving others without concerns about his bank balance. His life was full.

So what the hell was he doing here?

Ashley Carson was sexy, no question, her prettiness increased all the more by the way she didn't seem to realize her own appeal. Still, he worked around beautiful women all the time and held himself in check. Something he would continue to do when he retrieved his briefcase—and no, damn it, leaving it there wasn't a subconscious slip on his part. Matthew opened the sedan door—

And heard the smoke alarm *beep, beep, beeping* from inside the restaurant.

An even louder alert sounded in his head as a whiff of smoke brushed his nose. He scoured the lot. Her small blue sedan sat in the same spot it had when he'd left.

"Ashley?" he shouted, hoping she'd already come outside.

No answer.

His muscles contracted and he sprinted toward the porch while dialing 9-1-1 on his cell to call the fire department. He gripped the front doorknob, the metal hot in his hand. In spite of its scorching heat, he twisted the knob. Thank God she'd left it unlocked after he'd gone. The leash snapped on Matthew's restraint and he shoved into the lobby.

Heat swamped him, but he saw no flames in the old mansion's foyer.

Through the shadowy glow, the fire seemed contained to the gift shop and his feet beat a path in that direction. Flames licked upward from the racks of clothing in the small store. Paint bubbled, popped and peeled on aged wood.

"Ashley?" Matthew shouted. "Ashley!"

Bottles of perfume exploded. Glass spewed through the archway onto the wooden floor. Colognes ignited, feeding the blaze inside the gift shop.

He pressed deeper inside. Boards creaked and shifted, plaster falling nearby, all leading him to wonder about the structural integrity of the hundred-and-seventy-year-old house. How much time did he have to find her?

As long as it took.

His leather loafers crunched broken glass. "Ashley, answer me, damn it."

Smoke rolled through the hallway. He ducked lower, his arm in front of his face as he called out for her again and again.

Then he heard her.

"Help!" A thud sounded against the wall. "Anybody, I'm in here."

Relief made him dizzier than the acrid smoke.

"Hold on, Ashley, I'm coming," he yelled.

The pounding stopped. "Matthew?"

Her husky drawl of his name blindsided him. A gust of heat at his back snapped him back to the moment. "Keep talking."

"I'm over here, in the powder room."

Her hoarse tones drove Matthew the last few feet. The door rattled, then stopped. A handle lay on the ground. "Get as far away from the door as you can. I'm coming in."

"Okay," Ashley said, her raspy voice softer. "I'm out of the way."

Straightening, he slid his body into the suffocating cloud. He didn't have much time left. If the blaze snaked down the hall, it would tunnel out of control.

Matthew shoved with his shoulder, again, harder, but the door didn't budge, the old wood apparently sturdier than the handle. He took three steps back for a running start.

And rammed a final time. The force shuddered through him as finally the panel gave way and crashed inward.

He scanned the dim cubicle and found Ashley— thank God—sitting, wedged in a corner by the sink, wrapped in a wet blanket. Smart woman.

Matthew wove around the fallen door toward her. He sidestepped a broken chair, the whole room in shambles. She'd obviously fought to free herself. This subdued woman apparently packed the wallop of a pocket-size warrior.

"Thanks for coming back," she gasped out, thrusting out a hand with a dripping wet hand towel. "Wrap this around your face."

Very smart woman. He looped the cloth around his face, scarf style, to filter the air.

Ashley rose to her feet, coughed, gasped. Damn. She needed air, but she wouldn't be able to walk over the shards of glass and sparking embers with her bare feet.

He hunkered down, dipping his shoulder into her midsection and swooping her up. "Hang on."

"Just get us out of here." She hacked through another rasping cough.

Matthew charged through the shop, now more of a kiln. Greedy flames crawled along a counter. Packs of stationery blackened, disintegrated.

Move faster. Don't stop. Don't think.

A bookshelf wobbled. Matthew rocked on his heels. Instinctively, he curved himself over Ashley. The towering shelves crashed forward, exploding into a pyre, stinging his face. Blocking his exit.

His fist convulsed around the blanket. A burning wood chip sizzled through his leather shoe.

"The other entrance, through the kitchen," Ashley hollered through wrenching coughs and her fireproof cocoon. "To the left."

"Got it." Backtracking, he rounded the corner

into the narrow hall. The smoke thinned enough for light to seep through the glass door.

Ashley jostled against him, a slight weight. Relief slammed him with at least twice the force. Too damn much relief for someone he barely knew.

Suddenly the air outside felt as thick and heavy as the smoldering atmosphere back inside.

Ashley gasped fresh air by the Dumpster behind her store. Hysteria hummed inside her.

At least the humid air out here was fresher than the alternative inside her ruined restaurant. Soon to be her entirely ruined home if firefighters didn't show up ASAP and knock back the flames spitting through two kitchen windows.

The distant siren brought some relief, which only freed her mind to fill with other concerns. How could the blaze have started? Had one of the candles been to blame? How much damage waited back inside?

Matthew's shoulder dug into her stomach. Each loping step punched precious gasps from her and brought a painful reminder of her undignified position. "You can put me down now."

"No need to thank me," he answered, his drawl raspier. "Save your breath."

How could he be both a hero and an insensitive jerk in the space of a few hours?

Her teeth chattered. Delayed reaction, no doubt.

The fine stitching along the bottom of his Brooks Brothers suit coat bobbed in front of her eyes. The graveled parking lot passed below. Now that the imminent danger of burning to death had ended, she could distract herself with an almost equally daunting problem.

Earlier she'd bemoaned the fact Matthew hadn't seen her in the pink satin nightgown—and now she wished he could see her in anything but that scrap of lingerie underneath her soggy blanket.

"Matthew," Ashley squeaked. "I can walk. Let me go, please."

"Not a chance." He shifted her more securely in place. The move nudged the blanket aside, baring her shoulder. His feet pounded the narrow strip of pavement at a fast jog. "You're going straight to the hospital to be checked over."

"You don't need to carry me. I'm fine." She gagged on a dry cough, gripping the edges of the slipping blanket. "Really."

"And stubborn."

"Not at all. I just hate for you to wear yourself out." Except after last night she knew just how much stamina his honed body possessed.

She grappled with the edges of the wet afghan, succeeding only in loosening the folds further and nearly flipping herself sideways off Matthew's shoulder.

"Quit wiggling, Ashley." He cupped her bottom. *Oh, my.*

His touch tingled clear to the roots of her long red hair swishing as she hung upside down.

Two firefighters rounded the corner, dragging a hose as they sprinted past, reminding her of bigger concerns than the impact of Matthew's touch and her lack of clothing. Her restaurant was burning down, her business started with her two foster sisters in the only real home she'd ever known. The place had been willed to them by dear "Aunt" Libby who'd taken them in.

Tears clogged her nose until another coughing jag ripped through her. Matthew broke into a run. She gripped the hem of his jacket.

A second rig jerked to a halt in front. With unmistakable synergy, the additional firefighters shot into action. Oh God. What if the fire spread? A wasted minute could carry the blaze to the other historic, wooden structures lining the beachfront property. Her foster sister Starr even lived next door with her new husband.

The fire chief shouted clipped orders. A small crowd of neighbors swelled forward, backlit by the ocean sunrise.

"Ashley?"

She heard her name through the mishmash of noises. Turning her head, Ashley peeked through her curtain of hair to find her foster sister Starr pushing forward.

Ashley wanted to warn Starr to get back, but dizziness swirled. From hanging upside down, too much gasping, or too much Matthew, she couldn't tell. Lights from fire trucks and an EMS vehicle strobed over the crowd, making Ashley queasy. She needed to lie down.

She wanted out of Matthew's arms before their warmth destroyed more than any fire.

He halted by the gurney, cradling Ashley's head as he leaned forward. She should look away. And she would, soon. But right now with her head fuzzy from smoke inhalation, she couldn't help reliving the moment when he'd laid her on her bed. His deep emerald eyes had held her then as firmly as they did now. His lean face ended in a stubborn jaw almost too prominent, but saved from harshness by a dent dimpling the end.

In her world filled with things appealing to the eye, he still took the prize.

"Please, let me go," she whispered, her voice hoarse from hacking, smoke and emotion.

Matthew finished lowering her to the stretcher. "The EMS folks will take care of you now."

His hands slid from beneath her, a long, slow caress scorching her skin through the blanket. He stepped back, the vibrant June sunrise shimmering behind his shoulders.

Already edgy, she looked away, needing distance. Her burning business provided ample distraction. Smoke swelled through her shattered front window, belching clouds toward the shoreline. Soot tinged her wooden sign, staining the painstakingly stenciled *Beachcombers*.

What was left inside their beautiful home inherited from their foster mother? She and her two sisters had invested all their heart and funds to start Beachcombers. She raised herself on her elbows for a better view, sadness and loss weighting her already labored breathing.

"Ashley." Her sister—Starr—elbowed through to her side. She wrapped her in a hug, an awkward hug Ashley couldn't quite settle into and suddenly she realized why.

Starr was tugging the wet blanket back up. Damn. The satin nighty. Maybe no one else had seen.

Who was she kidding? She only hoped Matthew had been looking the other way.

Her eyes shot straight to him and… His hot gaze said it all. The jerk who'd walked out on her had suddenly experienced a change of heart because of her lingerie, not because of her.

Damn. She wanted her white cotton back.

Two

"Ashley?" Matthew blinked, half certain smoke inhalation must have messed with his head.

He blinked again to get a better view in the morning sun. Ashley was now covered back up in the blanket. Except one creamy shoulder peeked free with a pink satin strap that told him he'd seen exactly what he thought when the soggy covering slipped. Ashley Carson had a secret side.

Something he didn't want anyone else seeing. He angled his body between Ashley and the small gathering behind them.

A burly EMS worker waved him aside. "Back

up, please, Congressman. The technician over there will check on you while I see to this lady." The EMS worker secured an oxygen mask over Ashley's face, his beefy, scarred hands surprisingly gentle. "Breathe. That's right, ma'am. Again. Just relax."

Vaguely Matthew registered someone taking his vitals, hands cleaning his temple and applying a bandage. He willed his breathing to regulate, as if that could help Ashley. She needed to be in the hospital. He should be thinking of that, not last night.

A light touch on his sooty sleeve cut through his focus. Ashley's foster sister stood beside him— Starr Reis. He remembered her name from other political events hosted at Beachcombers. Long dark hair tumbled over her shoulders, her eyes crinkled with worry.

"Congressman? What happened in there?"

"I wish I knew." How had the place caught on fire so quickly? He hadn't been gone that long.

"If only I hadn't overslept this morning, maybe I would have heard the smoke alarm." Starr shifted from one bare foot to another, her paint-splattered shirt and baggy sleep pants all but swallowing the petite woman. "I just called David. He's on his way home from an assignment in Europe."

"I'm glad you could reach him." He recalled her Air Force husband worked assignments around the world. A photographic memory for faces and names came in handy on the campaign trail.

This had to be hell for the woman, seeing her sister in danger and watching her business burn. At least the flames hadn't spread next door to Starr's home.

"Thank you for going in there." Starr blinked back tears and shoved a hank of wild curls from her face. "We'll never be able to repay you."

Matthew tugged at his tie, too aware of Ashley a few inches away, close enough she could overhear. He doubted Starr would keep thanking him if she knew the full story about what had happened last night and how it had ended.

He settled for a neutral, "I'm just glad to have been in the right place at the right time."

"What amazing good luck you were around." Starr smoothed a hand over her sister's head. "Why were you here? Beachcombers doesn't open for another hour."

His eyes snapped to Ashley's. He didn't expect she would say anything here, now. But would she be sharing sister girl talk later? He sure as hell didn't intend to exchange locker-room confidences with anyone about this. Keeping his life private was tough enough with the press hounding him and everyone around him for a top-dollar tidbit of gossip.

Starr frowned. "Matthew?"

"I came by for—"

"He came to—" Ashley brushed aside Starr's hand and lifted the oxygen mask. "He needed to pick up contracts for the fund-raiser. Please, don't worry about me. What's going on with Beachcombers? Is that another police siren?"

She tugged the blanket tighter and tried to stand. No surprise. While he hadn't known Ashley for more than a few months, she clearly preferred people didn't make a fuss over her. A problem for her at this particular moment, because he wasn't budging until he heard the all-clear from her EMS tech.

Matthew turned to the burly guy who tucked a length of gauze back into a first-aid kit. "Shouldn't she be in a hospital?"

"Congressman Landis?" a voice called from behind him, drew closer, louder. "Just one statement for the record before you go."

Holy hell. He glanced over his shoulder and took in the well-dressed reporter holding a microphone, her cameraman scurrying behind her with a boom mike and video recorder. He recognized this woman as an up-and-coming scrapper of a journalist who was convinced he would be her ticket to a big story this election season.

How could he have forgotten to look out for the press, even here, at a restaurant buried in an exclusive stretch of beachside historic homes? He'd been a politician's son for most of his life. A South

Carolina congressman in his own right. Now a candidate for the U.S. Senate.

He might not always be able to keep his private life quiet, but he would make sure Ashley's stayed protected. He'd hurt her enough already.

Matthew pivoted and before he could finish saying, "No comment," he heard a camera click. So much for his resolve to close the book on his time with Ashley.

Showering in the hospital bathroom, Ashley finished lathering her soot-reeking hair and ducked her head under the spray. The *tap, tap, tap* of the water on green tile reminded her of the sound of cameras snapping photographs earlier. At least the EMS technicians had hustled her into the ambulance and slammed the doors before any members of the media could push past Matthew's barricading body.

Still, no matter how long she stood under the soothing spray, she couldn't wash away the frustration burning along her nerves. Matthew Landis had only blown through Charleston a few times and already he'd turned her life inside out, like a garment tugged off too quickly.

Had he really stared at her for a second too long when the blanket slipped? Part of her gloried in his wide-eyed expression, especially after his hasty retreat earlier that morning. Then tormenting images came to mind of him risking his life to save her when she'd been trapped in the powder room. Ashley grabbed the washcloth and scrubbed away the lingering sensation of smoke and Matthew's touch.

Once she'd dried off and wrapped her hair in a towel, she felt somewhat steadier. She slipped into the nightgown and robe her sister had brought by her hospital room, giving only a passing thought to the ruined pink peignoir. Yes, she was well on her way to putting the whole debacle behind her. She had more important things to concentrate on anyway—like the fiery mess. Ashley yanked open the bathroom door.

And stopped short.

Matthew Landis sat on the hospital room's one chair, stretching his legs in front of him. He wore a fresh gray suit with a silver tie tack that she could swear bore the South Carolina state tree—a palmetto. How he managed such relaxed composure—especially given today's circumstances—she would never know.

He appeared completely confident and unfazed by their near-death experience. The small square bandage on his temple offered the only sign he'd blasted into a burning building and saved her life.

Her throat closed up again as she thought of all that could have happened to him in that fire. She needed to establish distance from him. Fast.

He held a long-stemmed red rose in one hand. She refused to consider he'd brought it for her. He'd undoubtedly plucked it from one of the arrangements already filling the rolling tray and windowsill. He twirled the stem between his thumb and forefinger. Why had he stuck around Charleston rather than returning to his family's Hilton Head compound?

Ashley cinched the belt on her hospital robe tighter. Her other hand clutched the travel pack of shampoo, mouthwash and toothpaste. "I didn't, uh, expect...."

He didn't move other than a slow blink and two twirls of the flower. "I knocked."

She unwrapped the towel, her hair unfurling down her back. "Obviously I didn't hear you."

Silence mingled with the scent of all those floral arrangements. Matthew stood. Ashley backed up a step. She hooked the towel over the doorknob and looked everywhere but at his piercing green eyes that had so captivated constituents for years.

Everyone in this part of the country had watched the four strapping Landis brothers grow up in the news, first while their father occupied the senate. Then after their dad's tragic death, their mother had taken over his senatorial seat.

Matthew had followed in his family's footsteps by running for the U.S. House of Representatives after completing his MBA, and now that his mom was moving on to become the secretary of state, Matthew was campaigning for her vacated senate seat.

The name Landis equaled old money, privilege, power and all the confidence that came with the influential package. She wanted to resent him for being born into all of those things so far outside her reach. Except his family had always lived lives beyond reproach. They were known to be genuinely good people. Even their political adversaries had been hard-pressed to find a reason to criticize the Landises for much of anything other than their stubborn streak.

He cleared his throat. "Are you okay?"

She spun to face him. "I'm fine."

"Ashley." He shook his head.

"What?"

He stuffed his hands in his pockets. "I'm a politician. Word nuances don't escape me. 'Fine' means you're only telling me what I want to hear."

Why did he have to look so crisp and appealing while she felt disheveled and unsettled? The scene felt too parallel to the one they'd played out just this morning. "Well, I am fine all the same."

"It's good to hear that. What's the doctor's verdict?"

"Dr. Kwan says I can leave in the morning." She skirted around Matthew toward the bedside table to put away her toiletries. "He diagnosed a mild to moderate case of smoke inhalation. My throat's still a little raw but my lungs are fine. I have a lot to be grateful for."

"I'm glad you're going to be all right." Still he watched her with that steady gaze of his that read too much while revealing only what he chose.

"I've sucked down more cups of ice chips than I care to count. I'm lucky, though, and I know it. Thank you for risking your life to save me." She tightened the cap on her toothpaste, then rolled the end to inflate the thumbprint in the middle. The question she'd been aching to ask pushed up her throat just as surely as the toothpaste made its way toward the top of the tube. "Why did you come back this morning?"

"I forgot my briefcase." He set the flower aside on the rolling tray.

Her thumb pushed deeper into the tube of Crest. She looked down quickly so he wouldn't be able to catch her disappointment. "I hope you didn't have anything irreplaceable in there because I'm pretty sure that even if it didn't burn up, the papers are suffering from a serious case of waterlog."

She tried to laugh but it got stuck somewhere between her heart and her throat. For once, she was grateful for the cough that followed. Except she couldn't stop.

Matthew edged into sight, a cup of water in his hand. She took it from him, careful not to brush fingers, gripped the straw and gulped until her throat cleared.

Ashley sunk to the edge of the bed, gasping. "Thank you."

"I should have gotten you out faster." His brow furrowed, puckering the bandage.

"Don't be ridiculous. I'm alive because of you." Her bare feet swinging an inch from the floor, she crumpled the crisp sheets between her fingers to keep from checking the bandage on his temple. "Uh, how bad was the damage to Beachcombers? Starr gave me some information, but I'm afraid she might have soft-soaped things for fear of upsetting me."

He pulled the chair in front of her and sat. "The structure is intact, the fire damage appears contained to downstairs, but everything is going to be water-logged from the fire hoses. That's all I could tell from the outside."

"Inspectors will probably have more information for us soon."

"If they show any signs of giving you trouble, just let me know and I'll get the family lawyers on it right away."

"Starr said pretty much the same when she came by earlier. She just kept repeating how glad she is that I'm alive."

Their other foster sister, Claire, had echoed the sentiment when she'd called from her cruise with her husband and daughter. Insurance would take care of the cost. But Ashley still couldn't help feeling responsible. The fire had happened on her watch and she'd been so preoccupied with Matthew she may well have screwed up in some way. How could she help but blame herself?

Matthew shifted from the chair to sit beside her on the bed and pulled her close before she could think to protest. His fingers tunneling under her damp hair, he patted between her shoulder blades. Slowly, she relaxed against his chest, drawn by the now-familiar scent of his aftershave, the steady thud of his heart beneath his starched shirt. After a hellish day such as the one she'd been through, who could fault her for stealing a moment's comfort?

"It'll be okay," he chanted, his husky Southern drawl stroking her tattered nerves as surely as his hands skimmed over her back. "You've got plenty of people to help."

His jacket rasped against her cheek and she couldn't resist tracing the palmetto tree tie tack. Being in his arms felt every bit as wonderful as she remembered. And here they were again.

Could she have misread his early departure this morning? "Thank you for stopping by to check on me."

"Of course. And I was careful not to be seen."

Her heart stuttered and it had nothing to do with the whiff of his aftershave. "What?"

He smoothed her hair from her face, his strong

hands gentle along her cheeks. "I was able to dodge the media on my way inside the hospital."

She thought back to the barrage of questions shouted their way as she'd been loaded into the ambulance. Uneasily, she inched out of his arms. "I imagine there will be plenty of coverage of your heroic save."

Matthew scrubbed a hand along his jaw. "That's not exactly the angle the media's working."

Apprehension prickled along her spine nearly managing to nudge aside the awareness of his touch still humming through her veins. "Is there a problem?"

"Don't worry." His smile almost reassured her. Almost. "I'll take care of everything with the press and the photos that are popping up on the Internet. Once my campaign manager works his magic with a new spin, nobody will think for even a second that we're a couple."

Three

Not a couple? Wow, he sure could use some lessons on how to let a girl down easy.

Ashley shoved her palms against his chest. His big arrogant chest. So much for assuming he'd been attracted to her after all. It would be a cold day in hell before she fell into those mesmerizing eyes again. "Glad to hear you've got everything under control."

Matthew eased to his feet, confidence and that damned air of sincerity mucking up the air around him. "My campaign manager, Brent Davis, is top—"

Ashley raised a hand to stop him. "Great. I'm not surprised. You can handle anything."

He searched her with his gaze. "Is there something wrong? I thought you would be pleased to know about the damage control."

Damage control? Her experience with him fell under the header of freaking *damage* control? Her anger burned hotter than any fire.

But the last thing she needed was for him to get a perceptive peek into her emotions. She scrambled for a plausible excuse in case he picked up on her feelings. "I'm dreading going over to the store tomorrow, but at the same time can't wait to set things in order. It's a relief to know I don't have anything to worry about with the press." Damn it all, she was babbling now, but anything was better than an awkward silence during which she might do something rash—like punch him. "So that's that then."

He didn't leave, just stood, his brows knitting together. Her heart tapped an unsteady beat in spite of herself.

Okay, so he was *hot* and confident and sincere looking. And he didn't want her. She shouldn't be this pissed off. It was just an impulsive one-night stand. People did that sort of thing.

She just never had. But she wasn't totally inexperienced. Why then did a single lapse against his chest plummet her into a world of sensation that a bolt of silk couldn't hope to rival?

She wanted, needed, him gone now. "Thanks again for visiting, but I have to dry my hair."

Oh great. Really original brush-off line.

He massaged his temple beside the bandage. "Promise me you'll be careful. Don't rush into Beachcombers until you get official notice that it's safe."

"I pinky swear. Now you really can go." Why wouldn't he leave the hospital? Better yet, return to Hilton Head altogether.

"About this morning… Ah, hell." He stuffed his hands in his pockets. "You're still okay with everything. Right?"

Full-scale alert. The man was rolling out the pity party. How mortifying.

If he said anything more, she might well slug him after all, which would rumple his perfectly tailored suit and show far more than she wanted him to see concerning his effect over her. "I have bigger concerns in my life right now than thinking about bed partners."

"Fair enough."

"I have to deal with the shop, my sisters, insurance claims." She was a competent businesswoman and he should respect her for that. No pity.

"I've got it." He held up his hands, a one-sided smile crooking up. "You're ready for me to leave."

Sheesh. How had he managed to turn the tables so fast until she felt guilty? Blast his politician skills that made her feel suddenly witchy.

She softened her stance and allowed herself to smile benignly back. "Last night was…nice. But it's back to real life now."

He arched one aristocratic brow. "Nice? You think the time we spent naked together was *nice?*"

Uh-oh. She'd thrown down a proverbial gauntlet to a man who made a profession out of competition. A chill tightened her scalp.

She shuffled to the window, offering him her back until she could stare away the need to explore the heat in his eyes again. Her poise threatened to snap. Matthew's return had already left her raw, and today she had little control to spare.

"Matthew, I need for you to go *now.*" She toyed with the satin bow in a potted fern, the ribbon's texture reminding her of the gown she'd foolishly donned earlier.

"Of course." His voice rumbled, smoother than the ribbon in her hand or the fabric along her body.

Two echoing footsteps brought him closer. His breath heated through her hair. "I'm sorry about the media mess and for not keeping my distance when I should have. But there's not a chance in hell I would call last night something so bland as 'nice.'"

If he touched her again, she'd snap, or worse yet, kiss him.

Ashley spun to face him, the window ledge biting into her back. His gaze intense, glowing, he stared down at her. The bow crumbled in her clenched hand.

Forget courtesy. "My sister is on her way with a blow-dryer. She forgot to bring one when she brought by my other things."

He nodded simply. "Call me if you have any unexpected troubles with the press or the insurance company."

The door hissed closed behind him. Snatching up the rose he'd held, Ashley congratulated herself on not sprinting after him. Especially since her lips felt swollen and hungry. She'd always been attracted to him. What woman wouldn't be?

Her body wanted him. Her mind knew better—when she bothered to listen. She'd vowed she wouldn't be one of those females who lost twenty IQ points when a charming guy smiled.

She sketched the flower against her cheek, twirling the stem between two fingers. How would she manage to resist him now that she'd experienced just how amazing his touch felt on her naked skin?

Straightening her spine, she stabbed the long stemmed bud back into a vase. The same way she'd done everything else since her parents tossed her out before kindergarten.

With a steely backbone honed by years of restraint.

* * *

It took all his restraint not to blow a gasket when he saw the morning paper.

Matthew gripped the worst of the batch in his fist as he rode the service elevator up to Ashley's hospital room. He'd known the press would dig around. Hell, they had been doing so for most of his life. Overall, he took those times as opportunities to voice his opinions. Calmly and articulately.

Right now, he felt anything but calm.

He unrolled the tabloid rag and looked again at the damning photos splashed across the front page. Somehow, a reporter had managed to get shots of his night with Ashley. Intimate photos that left nothing to the imagination. The most benign of the batch? A picture of him with Ashley at her front door, when she'd been wearing her robe. When he'd leaned to kiss her goodbye.

The photographer had gerrymandered his way to just the right angle to make that peck on the cheek look like a serious liplock.

Then there was the worst of the crop. A telephoto-lens shot through one of the downstairs bay windows when he and Ashley had been in the hall, on their way to her room, ditching clothes faster than you could say "government cheese."

Had she seen or heard about the pictures yet? He would find out soon enough.

The elevator jolted to a stop. Door swished apart to reveal a nurse waiting for him with a speculative gleam in her matronly eyes. He managed not to wince and gestured for her to lead the way.

The nurse's shoes squeaked on the tile floors as he strode behind her, the sounds of televisions and a rattling food cart filling the silence as people stopped talking to stare when he walked past.

He understood well enough the ebb and flow of gossip in this business. For the most part, he could shrug it off. But he wasn't so sure someone as private and reserved as Ashley could do the same.

Matthew nodded his thanks to the nurse and knocked on Ashley's door. "It's me."

The already cracked open door swooshed wider. Ashley sat in the chair by the window, wearing jeans and two layered shirts, all of which cupped her curves the way his hands itched to do.

He shoved the door closed behind him.

Ashley nodded to the paper in his fist. "The political scoop of the year."

Well, that answered one question. She'd already seen the paper. Or watched TV. Or listened to the radio.

Hell. "I am so damn sorry."

"I assume your campaign manager hasn't rolled out of bed yet," she said quietly, as stiff as the industrial chair.

"He's been awake since the phone rang at 4:00 a.m. warning him this was coming."

"And you didn't think it would be prudent to give me a heads-up?" While her voice stayed controlled, her red hair—gathered in a long ponytail—all but crackled with pent-up energy as it swept over her shoulder, along her pink and green layered shirts.

"I would have called, but the hospital's switchboard is on overload."

She squeezed her eyes shut, a long sigh gusting past her lips. Finally, she unclenched her death grip on the chair's arms and looked at him again. "Why does the press care who you're sleeping with?"

She couldn't be that naive. He raised an eyebrow.

"Okay, okay." She shoved to her feet and started pacing restlessly around the small room. "Of course they care. They are interested in anything a politician does, especially a wealthy one. Still why should it matter in regards to the polls? You're young, unattached. I'm single and of legal age. We had sex. Big deal."

As she passed, a drying strand of hair fluttered, snagging on his cuff link and draping over his hand. Each movement of her head as she continued talking shifted the lock of hair without sliding it away.

Why couldn't he twitch the strand free? "You may or may not have read about how my last breakup ended badly. My ex-girlfriend didn't take it well when I ended things and she let that be known in the press. Of course the media never bothered to mention she was cheating while I was in D.C."

Her answer dimly registered in his mind as he stared while the overhead light played with the hints of gold twining through the red lock. He kept his arm motionless. The strand slashed across his hand the way her hair had played along his chest when she'd leaned over him, her beautiful body on display for him.

Naked.

He cleared his throat and his thoughts. He needed to prepare her for what she would face once she left this room. "The media are going to hound you for details. You can't comprehend how intense the scrutiny will be until you've lived with it. Do you have any idea how many reporters are out there waiting for a chance to talk to you right now?"

"When my sister gets here, we'll slip out the back entrance." She eyed the door with a grimace. "I'm sure the hospital staff will be happy to help."

He scratched behind his ear. "It's not that simple. And your sister's not coming."

She pointed to his hand. "Stop scratching."

What the hell? "Pardon?"

"Scratching. It's your poker tell. You only do that when you're trying to think of a way around a question. What are you hiding—" She paused, scowled. "Wait. You told my sister not to come, didn't you?"

Matthew dropped his arm to his side. Damn it, he'd never realized he had a "tell" sign. Why hadn't he or his campaign manager picked up on that before? At least Ashley had alerted him so he could make a conscious effort to avoid it in the future.

Meanwhile, he had to deal with a fired-up female. "Her husband and I thought it would be safer for her to stay out of the mob outside."

"You and David decided? You two have been as busy as your campaign manager." She scooped up her overnight tote bag. "I'll take a cab."

Matthew eased the canvas sack from her hand before she could hitch the thing over her shoulder. "Don't be ridiculous. My car is parked right by the back exit."

Her eyes battled with him for at least a three count before she finally sighed. "Fine. The sooner we go the sooner this will be past us."

A short ride down the elevator later, he opened the service entrance—and found four photographers poised and ready. He shielded Ashley as best he could and hustled her into his car. More pictures of the two of them wouldn't help matters, but better he be there to move this along than having her face them alone.

He plowed past a particularly snap-happy press

hound and slid into the driver's side of his Lexus, closing the door carefully, but firmly after him.

Ashley sagged in her seat. "God, you're right. I didn't realize it would be this bad."

"Bad?" He gunned the gas pedal. "I hate to tell you, but we got off easy, and they're not going to give up anytime soon. They will pry into every aspect of your private life."

Her face paled, but she sat up straighter. "I guess I'll just have to invest in some dark glasses and really cool hats."

He admired her spunk, even more so because he knew how much harder this was for her than it would be for others. "The press isn't going to leave you alone. They've been trying to marry me off for years."

"I'm tough," she said with only a small quiver in her voice. "I can wait it out."

Except she shouldn't have to. This was his fault and he should be the one bearing the fallout. Not her.

Then the answer came to him in a sweep of inspiration as smooth as the luxury car's glide along the four-lane road. Hadn't he already noted how much easier managing the media would be for her with him by her side? He knew the perfect way to keep her close *and* tamp down the negative gossip.

Decision made, he didn't question further, merely forged ahead. "There's a simpler way to make this die down faster."

"And that would be?" She swiped her palms over her jeans again and again, her frayed nerves all the more obvious with each passing palmetto and pine tree.

Stopping for a traffic light, he hitched his arm along the seat behind her head and pinned her with his most persuasive gaze. "We'll get engaged."

"Engaged?" Her eyes went wide and she jerked away from the brush of his arm as if scorched. "You've got to be kidding. Don't you think getting married to pacify the press is a little extreme?"

Marriage. The word stabbed through him like a well-sharpened blade. He absolutely agreed with her point about staying clear of the altar.

The light turned green and he welcomed the chance to shift his eyes back to the road. "It won't go that far. Once the buzz dies down and they focus on the issues again, you and I will quietly break up. We can simply turn the tables and state that the pressure from so much media attention put a strain on our relationship."

Yeah, the idea of lying chafed more than a little since he considered his ethics to be of the utmost importance. But right now, only one thing dominated his thoughts.

Keeping Ashley's reputation from suffering for his mistake.

He would have to live with the fallout from that,

not her. This was the best way to protect her. "We'll set up a press conference of our own to make the official announcement."

She crossed her arms over her chest, her brown eyes glinting nearly black with a determination that warned him he may have underestimated the strength of the woman beside him.

"Congressman Landis, you are absolutely out of your flipping mind. There's not a chance in hell you're putting an engagement ring on my finger."

Four

Uh-oh. She'd thrown down the proverbial gauntlet again.

Ashley gripped the sides of the butter-soft leather seat. She couldn't miss the competitive gleam in Matthew's eyes as he drove the luxurious sedan.

"Matthew," she rushed to backtrack. "I appreciate that you're concerned for my reputation, but one night of sex does not make me your responsibility. And it doesn't make *you* my responsibility, either."

He reached across to loosen her grip and link hands as they sped down the road. She looked away and tried to focus on the towering three-story homes, their deep porches sheltering rocking chairs and ferns. Anything to keep from registering how Matthew's thumb brushed back and forth across the sensitive inside of her wrist.

His callused thumb rasped against her tender skin, bringing to mind thoughts of all those photos of him in the paper featuring the numerous times he'd worked on Habitat homes. He came by the roughened skin and muscles the honest way. Her traitorous heart picked up pace from just his touch, a pulse he could no doubt feel.

Yep, there he went smiling again.

She snatched her hand away and tucked it under her leg. "Stop that. The last thing we need is to provide more photo ops for gossip fodder."

"Be my fiancée." He stated, rather than asking.

"No."

"I'll make it worth your while." He winked.

She covered her ears. "I am Ashley Carson and I do *not* approve this message."

Laughing, he gripped one of her wrists and lowered her arm. "Cute."

"And hopefully understood."

"Ashley, you're a practical woman, an accountant for God's sake. Surely you can see how this is the wisest course of action."

Practical? He wanted her for "practical" reasons? How romantic.

"Thanks, but I'll take my chances with the press." She tried to tug free her recaptured hand.

No such luck.

He held on and teased her with more of those understated but potent touches all the way to her sister's house—which just happened to have a red-and-blue Landis For Senate sign on the front lawn. Ashley shifted her attention to Beachcombers instead. And gasped from the shock and pain.

The sight in front of her doused passion and anger faster than if she'd jumped into the crashing surf in front of them. Beachcombers waited for her like a sad, bedraggled friend. Soot streaked the white clapboard beside broken windows, now boarded over. The grassy lawn was striped with huge muddy ruts from fire trucks and the deluge of water.

If she kept staring, she would cry. Yet, looking away felt like abandoning a loved one. She had bigger problems than her reputation—or some crazy mixed-up need to jump back into bed with a man certain to complicate her life.

She needed to regroup after the devastation, to meet with her sisters and revise her whole future. And no matter what plan they came up with, Matthew Landis would not be figuring into the strategy.

This time, when she pulled her hand back, she would make sure he understood that no meant no.

* * *

Waiting for Starr to come downstairs, Ashley peered through the living room window, watching as Matthew drove away.

A marriage proposal. Her first, and what a sham. Now that she'd gotten over the shock of his *faux* fiancée proposition, she had to appreciate that he wanted to preserve her reputation. An old-fashioned notion, certainly, but then his monied family was known for their by-the-rules manners. How ironic that Starr belonged in this kind of world for real now that she'd married into an established Charleston family.

The Landis's Hilton Head compound might be more modern than this place—she'd pored over a photo spread in *Southern Living*—but his home proclaimed all the wealth and privilege of this Southern antebellum house that had been in Starr's husband's family for generations.

Her artsy sister had put her own eclectic stamp on the historic landmark, mixing dark wood antiques with fresh new and bright prints. All the dour drapes had been stripped away and replaced with pristine white shutters that let in light while still affording privacy when needed.

Like now.

Ashley wandered across the room past the Steinway grand piano to the music cabinet beside it. Photos in sterling-silver frames packed the top. One of Starr and David on their wedding day. Another of David's mother perched royally in a wingback chair holding her cat.

And yet another of Starr, Claire and Ashley standing in front of the Beachcombers sign when they'd officially opened the business three years ago. Most restaurants failed in the first year, but they had defied the odds despite having no restaurant experience. Their clientele swelled as Charleston's blue-blooded brought their well-attended bridal breakfasts and showers to Beachcombers, drawn by hosting their events in such a scenically placed historic home.

Once Starr lured them in with her decorative eye for creating the perfect ambiance, their sister Claire's catering skills sealed the deal and Ashley tallied the totals. Their foster mother may have used up her entire family fortune taking in children, but she'd left a lasting legacy of love.

Ashley cradled a picture of Aunt Libby.

Their foster mother had lost her fiancé in the Korean War and pledged never to marry another man. Instead, she'd stayed in her childhood house and used all her inheritance to bring in girls who needed a home. Many had come and gone, adopted or returned to their parents. Just Claire, Starr and Ashley had stayed.

God, how she missed Aunt Libby. She could sure

use some of her cut-to-the-chase wisdom right about now. Aunt Libby had never cared what other people thought about her, and heaven knew there had been some hateful things said when Libby brought some of her more troubled teens to this high-end neighborhood

The light tread of footsteps on the stairs pulled her from her thoughts. Ashley turned to find her fireball of a sister sprinting toward her.

"Welcome! I'm so sorry I wasn't here to greet you."

"Not a problem." Ashley stepped into the familiar hug. This woman was as dear to her as any biological sibling ever could be. "Your housekeeper said you've been battling the stomach flu. Are you okay?"

"Nothing to worry about. I'm fine." Starr stepped back and hooked an arm through Ashley's. "Let's go up to my room. I've been sorting through my clothes to find some you can borrow until you get your closet restocked. I'm shorter than you are, but there are a few things that should work."

Starr pulled her sister up the stairs and into her bedroom…and holy cow, she'd meant it when she said she went through all her clothes. The different piles barely left any room to walk, turning the space into a veritable floordrobe.

"Really, you're being too generous. I don't want to put you out."

Starr smiled and slid her hand over her stomach. "Don't worry. I won't be able to fit in my clothes soon anyway. I don't have the stomach flu."

The hint flowered in her mind, stirring happiness and, please forgive her, a little jealousy. "You're pregnant?"

Starr nodded. "Two-and-a-half months. David and I haven't told anyone yet. I would have said something sooner, but it was totally a shock. We weren't planning to start a family yet, but I'm so happy."

"Of course you are. Congratulations." Ashley folded her in a hug. "I'm thrilled for you."

And she was. Truly. Both of her sisters were moving on with their lives, building families. She just wanted the same for herself. Someday. With a man who wasn't proposing a "practical" engagement.

Her sister held tight for a second before pulling back. "Okay, so?"

"So what?"

Starr picked up a newspaper on her bed stand and flopped it open. "Holy crap, kiddo, I can hardly believe my eyes. *You* slept with Matthew Landis?"

"Thanks for the vote of confidence." She knew she wasn't Matthew's type, but it hurt hearing her sister's incredulity. For that matter, why in the world would Matthew think the press would even believe an engagement announcement?

"I'm simply surprised because it's so sudden. I didn't realize you two had known each other that long." She folded the paper to cover the incriminating pictures. "Although given these, I guess you've been keeping a lot from me lately. I can't believe you didn't say anything when I brought the clothes to the hospital." There was no missing the hurt in her tone.

"I'm sorry and you're right—about the not knowing each other part. You already heard or read most of what there is to tell. We've seen each other during the course of planning functions and smaller gatherings for his campaign. That night, was just… well…"

"Spontaneously human?"

"Neither one of us was doing much thinking."

"Well, I'm glad you're all right."

"But?"

"It's such a tight race." Her sister picked at a pile of sparkly painted T-shirts that looked designer made yet had been created by artsy Starr. "I'd hate for his opponent to get any kind of leg up at a time when even a few votes can make a difference. There are some important issues at stake—like Martin Stewart's history in the state legislature and how he has hacked away funds that feed into the foster-care system."

Certainly discussion of the race had been bandied about among Beachcombers clientele with everyone weighing in. Ashley and her sisters had gotten behind Matthew early on given their strong stance on foster care. "That issue hits close to home, no question. But I'm sure the voters will see Martin Stewart for the phony snake he is by the time the campaign runs its course. The guy does the Potomac Two-Step changing his stance on issues so often he's a prime candidate for *Dancing With the Stars*."

Starr's packing slowed to a near halt. "I wish I could be so certain."

"I truly believe that. Remember when you worked after school in his office? It only took you a couple of months to quit that job. You said he was hell to work for. If you sensed that at seventeen surely older more mature voters will figure it out, too."

Starr resumed stacking piles in the box, quietly. Too quietly. Her sister never ran out of things to say.

Ashley tried to catch her sister's eye. "What's wrong?"

Starr pivoted on her heel, her eyes awash with pain—and anger. "I didn't quit that job. I was fired."

"Oh my God, why?"

"Because I wouldn't sleep with him."

Whoa. The impact of Starr's revelation set Ashley back a step. Then another until she sagged into a chair. "You were only seventeen. He must have been in his thirties then."

"Yeah, exactly." Starr stalked around the room,

dodging piles of clothes. "He fired me, and to top it off, just before that I had asked him to write a recommendation for me to get into that art school in Atlanta. Well, afterward, he made a call that ruined any chance I had at the scholarship."

"Starr, that's horrible." Ashley tried to hide her hurt that her sister hadn't shared something so life critical with her before now, but her firebrand of a sister seemed suddenly fragile. Plus she didn't want to upset a pregnant woman, so Ashley settled for, "I'm surprised Aunt Libby didn't string him up by his toenails."

She smoothed her hand along a bright red angora sweater with jet beads along the neckline, wondering how her vibrant sister had put up with that kind of treatment.

"I didn't tell her. I was embarrassed and—" Starr shrugged a shoulder "—afraid no one would believe me since my parents had been such scam artists. Then as time passed, it seemed best to just put it all behind me. I may seem more outgoing than you, but in those days it was mostly bravado."

Ashley hugged her again, holding on until her sister stopped shaking. "I'm so, so sorry you had to go through that."

Starr inched away and swiped her wrist across her eyes, bracelets jangling a discordant tune. "I could go to the press now, but since I'm your sister…"

"They would assume you're lying to help me out." Which would only make things worse.

"I'm afraid so. Maybe now you understand better why I've been so active in campaigning for Matthew Landis."

What a mess. If Matthew lost the election because of one night of consensual sex between two adults, that would be horribly unjust, but she knew well enough that life wasn't always fair. She had to do something to clean up the mess she'd made. She had to do something for Starr.

The obvious answer sat there in front of her in the way her sister had supported her and been the family she never had. She would do anything for the sisters who'd been so self-sufficient they didn't need much of anything from the youngest of their clan. "Don't worry about it. The press will have plenty to talk about before long."

"What do you mean?"

Ashley sucked in a bracing breath. "You aren't the only one with big news today. Matthew and I are engaged."

She would tell Matthew her decision to go forward with the engagement. Soon, since she'd called and asked him to stop by and pick her up for a late supper after she looked through the charred mess.

Her life would be changing at the speed of light

once she accepted his proposal. Even though she would be staying at Starr's during the Beachcomber renovations, Ashley knew the announcement would bring down a hailstorm of media attention. She only needed a few minutes alone inside her old world first—however wrecked it might be.

The air was heavy with humid dew. Ashley climbed the rear entrance steps toward the only real home she'd ever known while crickets chirped. At least the press couldn't get too close to her in the gated backyard. She panned her flashlight around the lawn and didn't see anyone lurking in the bushes.

Rubbing a hand over the creamy colored clapboard, she thought of the hours she'd spent developing the business with her sisters. A deep breath later, she pushed on the door. It stuck until an extra jolt of her shoulder nudged it loose.

The acrid pall nearly choked her. Who would have thought the smell could linger so long? Soot mingled in the air, hanging on the humidity like whispery spider webs.

No doubt, even walking through her shop would be messy, so Ashley tied her hair through itself into a loose slipknot. A quiver of dread fluttered to life. She squashed it before it could rob her of the drive she needed to face the damage.

A soaked rug squished beneath her shoes as she padded down the hallway. Pausing at her office, she tapped the door open, sighing to find all intact. A film of black residue smudged the surfaces of desks and shelves, but just as Matthew had promised, no fire damage.

She would come back to it later. First, she needed to confront the worst. Each step bubbled gray water from beneath her shoes, the squelching sound weakly echoing memories of Matthew's leather loafers pounding down the hall as he'd carried her.

Around the corner waited the main showroom. The horrid sense of helplessness returned, crawling between her shoulder blades like a persistent bug she couldn't swat away. Above all, Ashley hated feeling powerless.

She shook off the wasted emotion. Time to take control and face the nightmare so she could wake up and get her life back. Ashley plowed around the corner and into a broad male chest. She jumped back with a scream, slipping on the squishy rug.

But it wasn't the paparazzi.

Matthew filled the doorway. Apparently she would be talking to him sooner than she'd expected.

"Hold on a minute, darlin'." Matthew gripped her shoulders, his voice rumbling into the silence. "It's just me."

"Matthew, of course it's you." Shuddering with

relief, she instinctively sagged against him—then stiffened defensively.

He pulled her firmly against him anyway until she could only hear the steady thrum of his heart pulsing beneath her ear. His musky scent encircled her, insulating her from the fiery aftermath.

Her skin burned with a prickly sensation, almost painful. A rush of heat deep in the pit of her stomach made her long to melt against him, press her breasts to his chest until the ache subsided, or exploded into something magnificent.

Ashley flatted her palms on his chest and shoved. "You scared the hell out of me."

"Sorry." Matthew squished back a step, hands raised in surrender, his flashlight casting a dome of light. "I saw you crossing the yard and I came in through the front."

"It's okay. Now that I can breathe." It wasn't fair that she felt like death warmed over and he looked so damned good. Even in khakis and a polo shirt, he rippled with power.

Still, she felt tired and cranky, and his appeal left her edgy and vulnerable. She didn't like it—and she still had to tell him they were engaged after all. "What are you doing here so early?"

"You said you were coming to check out the damage." He absently scratched behind his ear, then stopped. "I thought you could use some help."

Miffed with herself for losing her temper, Ashley reined in her wayward emotions. She'd never used anger to get her way before. She couldn't see any reason to start now. Must be nerves from what she had to tell him.

She'd wanted a good night's sleep to brace herself, but so much for wishes. "I apologize and you're right, I did need to speak with you. We can talk while I do my walk-through of the place."

For the first time since she'd slammed into Matthew, his poster-boy-perfect mask slid. Concern wrinkled his brow. "Are you sure you're ready for this? Hire a clean-up crew and spare yourself some heartache."

"I'm not going to clean the place yet. Actually, I can't until the insurance company completes its assessment. I just wanted to look. It shouldn't take long."

He stepped aside. She gasped.

The whole room loomed like a black hole, void of color. Boards over the window even kept out much of the streetlights from lending any relief to the drab grays. Maybe she should have waited until morning after all and seen the place in the light of day. Surely the dark made everything seem worse than it was.

But probably not.

She'd hosted so many beautiful pre-wedding events here in the past, imagining celebrating her own engagement someday. What a crummy, crummy way to get her wish.

Matthew wondered how Ashley could stand so stoically still in the face of such a damn mess.

The second she'd told him she planned to come here, he'd known he would have to be there with her. For safety's sake and for support.

Her chin quivered. Totally understandable. He'd expected just such a reaction. He hadn't anticipated how her sadness would sucker punch him.

Matthew crossed his arms, trapping his hands so he wouldn't reach for her. She eased past him, the sweep of her peasant top brushing against his arm. What did she have on underneath? His throbbing body begged him to discover the answer.

Odd how he'd never considered that practical Ashley might wear her merchandise. Her merchandise. How could he have been so focused on thoughts of getting Ashley naked that he momentarily forgot about the mess around them?

Clothing racks lay on their sides, having been tipped by the force of spraying water. Curled wisps of melted fabrics stuck to the floor and hangers. That same material could have melted to her skin.

Matthew heard a bell chime behind him, followed by Ashley's chuckle. Her laugh rippled over his taut nerves, just as enticing as any slip. Damn. He was in trouble. "What did you find?"

Ashley reached inside the antique gilded cash register and pulled out a soggy stack of bills. "A few blasts with the blow-dryer and I'll be solvent."

Only Ashley could stand in the middle of a charred-out room, holding what probably amounted to a couple of hundred bucks and still manage a laugh.

He stepped deeper into the room. "So supper's on you tonight."

"Sure. I could probably afford to spring for burgers, if you don't mind splitting the Coke?"

"How about I give you some money, just to tide you over?"

Her pride blazed brighter than their two flash-lights combined. "I'll be fine once the insurance check arrives. I don't mind working off my deductible with sweat equity."

"It's a standing offer."

"Thanks, but no."

Matthew bit short a rebuttal. He could see she wouldn't be budged. He would just find other ways around her counterproductive need for independence. "All right then."

He followed her back down the hall, her gathered long hair swaying with each step baring a patch of her neck, and just that fast he started forgetting about the charred mess around them.

Until they reached her open bedroom door.

What if she'd been asleep in her bed when the fire started and he hadn't returned? Being inside the dressing room could very well have saved her life.

His chest tightened, his breathing ragged. He braced a forearm against the fire-split molding. His arms trembled with the tension of bunched muscles as he fought the image of Ashley dead.

She made a slow spin around to face him again. "Well, you were right, Matthew. There's not much I can do here for now. I feel better, though. Knowing the worst somehow makes it easier to go forward."

"Right." He only half registered her words, still caught in the hellish scenario of her stuck in this place while it burned. Thank God she wasn't his fiancée, someone like Dana who could wreck his world in a stopped heartbeat.

"I accept."

Ashley's words snapped him back to the present.

"Accept the money?" He was surprised, but damn glad. "Of course. How much do you need?" His eyes swept over her, unable to read her body language but sensing the tension coiling through her.

"Not that. I accept your, uh—" she chewed her lip "—your proposal. If you still think it will help your campaign, I'll be your fiancée."

Five

He was engaged. Hell.

Matthew creaked back in the chair at his bustling campaign headquarters in Hilton Head. Even four hours after Ashley's official acceptance, he still couldn't believe she had actually agreed. He'd gotten his way, but still the whole notion had him itching with the same sensation that had urged him to get out of her place as quickly as he could after their night together.

He stared at the computer screen full of briefing notes in front of him, but it registered as vaguely as the ringing of telephones and hum of the copy machine outside his office.

Thumbing the edge of a shiny red and blue stack of "Landis for Senate" bumper stickers, Matthew wondered why the thought of even a fake engagement floored him so much. After all, he'd gotten exactly what he wanted from her. It wasn't real like with Dana.

He just hadn't expected Ashley to be so damn reluctant in her agreement. Okay, so yeah maybe his ego smarted a little. *He* was the one who wanted to keep his bachelor life.

Wouldn't his brothers enjoy yucking it up over this mess?

A light tap sounded on his open door. He glanced up to find his campaign manager—Brent Davis—filling the opening. "Are you getting enough sleep?"

"You're kidding, right?" Matthew waved Brent to take the chair in front of the mahogany desk.

Older than Matthew by twenty years, the wiry manager had been an energetic force behind Matthew's mother's campaign and had acted as a consultant when Matthew ran for the House of Representatives. Brent had been the natural choice to head the campaign when Matthew made his decision to seek his mother's vacated senatorial seat.

For the first time, Matthew wondered if he'd decided to push too hard, too fast, politically. He could have hung out in the House for another ten years or so and still been on track to run for the senate by the time he was forty. But he'd been so hell-bent on not letting go of the seat that started with his father before shifting to his mom. He'd worried that someone else might get a lock on the spot that couldn't be broken.

Had his ambition pushed him to sacrifice anything—including an innocent person like Ashley?

Damn it all, he was doing this to help preserve her reputation. He'd made his decision and he wouldn't hurt her worse by changing his mind and offering her a trip to the Bahamas to hide out until the frenzy died out. While yes, he could have handled the scandal, it would have been a hell of a lot more taxing on everyone in his campaign who had worked so hard to get him here.

Time to step up to the plate and be a man. He leaned forward on his arms, shirtsleeves rolled up, and looked Brent Davis square in the eye. "Ashley Carson and I are engaged."

His campaign manager froze—no expression, no movement, not so much as a blink to betray his thoughts. Matthew knew from experience the guy only did that when he'd been tossed a curve ball that whacked him upside the skull. The last time Matthew had seen that look on Brent's face, he'd gotten the news flash that Ginger Landis had decided to elope with her longtime friend General Hank Renshaw during a goodwill tour across Europe.

Finally, Brent templed his pointer fingers and tapped them against his nose. "You're joking."

"I'm serious." Matthew straightened, unflinching.

One blink from Brent. Just one, but a fast flick of irritation. "You're engaged to the mouse of a girl in the compromising photos."

Anger blazed hot and fast. "Watch how you talk about Ashley."

Brent's eyes went wide. "Whoa, okay, take it down a notch there, big fella. I hear you loud and clear. You're totally in lust with this female."

"Davis…" Matthew growled his final warning.

Besides, the last thing he needed right now was to dwell on that night with Ashley, a train of thoughts guaranteed to steal what cool he had left at the moment. "She's my fiancée, my choice, deal with it. That's your job."

"Why didn't you tell me you were dating her when those damning photos hit the news?" Brent flattened his palms on the desk. "You left me to spin one helluva nightmare with incomplete informati— Wait." He leaned back with narrowed laser eyes. "This is one of those fake deals, isn't it? The two of you are making this up to get the heat off."

"I never said that," he hedged, unwilling to expose Ashley to any more embarrassment.

"You need to be honest with me if I'm going to help you make it through the November elections on top." Brent tapped the stack of bumper stickers with his pointer finger repeatedly for emphasis. "In fact, you should have told me before you proposed to her in the first place."

On the one hand, Matthew could see his point. On the other, it seemed damned ridiculous—not to mention unromantic—to clear his bridal choice with his campaign manager first.

If he were really getting married. Which he wasn't. But that was beside the point.

He wouldn't sacrifice Ashley to the media hyenas just to win an election. In spite of all his competitive urges that totally agreed with Brent, Matthew couldn't bring himself to say anything that might bring Ashley further embarrassment.

Something deep inside him insisted if he was the kind of man to abandon her, then he didn't deserve to win. "Ashley and I were work acquaintances who were surprised to find there was something more. Call it a whirlwind romance in your press release."

Brent nodded his head slowly, a smile spreading across his angular face for the first time since he'd entered the office. "If we put that out there to the media, then everyone will understand when the two of you decide to break off the impetuous engagement."

"I never said that, either."

"Damn it, Matthew—" his smile went wry "—I

taught you how to use those avoidant answer tech-niques with the press back when your mother was running for office. Don't think you can get away with using those same techniques on me."

Why couldn't he bring himself to close the office door and tell Brent the truth? It all came back to pro-tecting Ashley, her reputation and her pride as best he could until he set things right again in her life.

Matthew angled forward with a long creak of the wheels on the antique leather chair he'd inherited from his father. "I said Ashley and I are engaged and that's exactly what I mean. We're going to pick out a ring tomorrow."

A ring?

Hell yeah.

Of course they would need a ring. If Ashley balked, he would suggest they could sell it after-ward and donate the proceeds to her favorite charity. Ashley with all her generous ways would get into a notion like that. He wasn't actually purchasing any token of commitment, rather protecting Ashley while contributing to a worthy cause.

Brent eyed him narrowly. "Why not give this Ashley Carson woman your mother's ring from her marriage to your father?"

Good question.

"Ashley wants her own," he neatly dodged. "As a foster child, she lived her life receiving hand-medowns from others, rarely getting the chance to choose what suited *her* best. She deserves to have a ring of her choice and start traditions of her own."

Yeah, that sounded plausible enough, especially given he'd only had half a second to come up with an answer. As a matter of fact, it actually resonated as true inside him, the decision he would reach if he and Ashley were doing this couple thing for real.

Matthew aligned the stack of bumper stickers. "I imagine the news will leak from someone in the jewelry store, but we'll still want to make our own official announcement. When do you think is best to call a press conference? Tomorrow night or the next morning?"

"You actually love this woman?" His manager didn't even bother hiding the jaded tone in his voice.

Love? The word brought to mind the endless times he'd heard his mother crying on the other side of the door after Benjamin Landis's death. Ginger had been damn near incapacitated. If it hadn't been for her kids and the surprise offer to take over her husband's senate seat, Matthew still wasn't sure how long it would have taken his mother to enter the world of the living again.

He would have chalked it up to emotions growing over a long-term relationship, but he'd felt much the same crippling pain when his fiancée died in college. No way was he going back for round two of that pathway to hell. The possibility of letting anyone have that kind of control over him again scared the crap out of him.

He'd been right to try and end things after their accidental night together. Circumstances, however, had forced them to bide their time before going their separate and diverse ways.

He thought about Ashley, and yeah, she stirred a protectiveness inside him along with that hefty dose of arousal. Just thinking about her naked body tangled in the sheets with her auburn hair splayed over the pillow…

Damn. He wouldn't be standing up from behind the protective cover of his mahogany desk anytime soon. "I am captivated by her."

Brent stared him down and Matthew held his gaze without wavering. Finally, his old family friend nodded. "Either you're a brilliant liar or in more trouble than you realize, my friend."

The camera flash blinded her.

Ashley blinked to clear the sparks of light as the intense reflection bounced off the marquise-cut diamond on her finger as she stood in front of the podium outside Matthew's campaign headquarters in Hilton Head.

She hadn't wanted him to spend so much on the ring, but he'd swayed her by telling her the proceeds from hocking the rock afterward would go to the charity of her choice. That he knew her and her wishes so well after such a short time swayed her more than anything.

His campaign manager, Mr. Davis, stepped between them and the microphone. "Thank you, ladies and gentlemen of the press. That officially concludes our conference for this afternoon."

Ashley forced a smile on her face as cameras continued to click while Matthew escorted her toward a chauffeur-driven Suburban. The weight of the stone on her hand provided a constant reminder that while she might not be committed to this man, she was committed to her decision to help him with his campaign to beat his scumbag opponent.

She extended her fingers and stared at the brilliant diamond in the shiny gold setting, thought of their night together, followed by his cageyness the next morning.

She feared she'd made a mistake.

Not in deciding on the engagement. She still believed in making sure that rat bastard running against him didn't get to exploit anyone else.

But this ring? She turned her hand to catch fragments of sunlight in the facets of the stone. The ring was perfect, exactly what she would want in a real engagement and now she could never have it because the marquise cut would always remind her of Matthew Landis and the way he'd hurt her.

She couldn't help but think of how he'd hotfooted toward her door. When this relationship didn't benefit him anymore, he would likely hotfoot his way out of her life just that fast. She didn't want to view him in such an unfavorable light, but what else could she think? That's what he'd shown her, and he *was* a politician, after all.

Although she'd seen signs he wasn't the typical politician, she reminded herself he was used to spinning things to his own advantage. She needed to remember that in order to survive this debacle.

Ashley slid into the backseat of the Suburban, the driver closing the door after her while she settled into the decadently soft leather. A built-in television played a twenty-four hour news channel.

Matthew tossed his briefcase to the floor before buckling his seat belt. "Thank God, that's past. We should have some time to talk before we reach my place."

Her ears perked up and she lost focus on the ring. "Your place?"

"Yes, you should familiarize yourself with the property." He angled to face her, his knee brushing against hers and stirring more than nerves in her stomach. "It would seem strange if you're unfamiliar with where I live."

"Of course. That makes sense." She forced her face to stay blasé even though inside she couldn't ignore the frustrated twinge that his reasons for taking her home were merely practical. "Why didn't your campaign manager come along then? Where is he now?"

"Don't know." Matthew shrugged as a golf course with a lush lawn and palm trees whizzed past.

"I thought he wanted to tell me more about the upcoming agenda." She tugged her lightweight sweater closed over her floral sundress she'd borrowed from Starr. The outfit was pretty, but Starr wasn't as busty so the darn thing didn't fit quite right and the press of Matthew's knee against hers was starting to make the dress even more uncomfortably tight as her breasts ached for his touch.

She should have been shopping for clothes rather than a ring in order to pull off this charade.

"Brent and I decided I could give you the information just as easily. He has enough to keep him busy." Matthew clicked open his briefcase and pulled out a printed agenda roster. "I'm slated to speak at a Rotary breakfast in the morning and a stump gathering in the afternoon. On Saturday evening, there's a harbor cruise fund-raising dinner."

He paused reading to glance over at her, seemingly unaware of the havoc he wreaked on her senses with just the touch of his kneecap, for Pete's sake. If only the photographers hadn't caught those compromising photos, she could have gone on with her life, pissed off at him, certainly, but free of this painful attraction.

"Ashley?" He ducked his head into her line of sight. "Are you with me? Do you have a problem with any of this? You don't have to attend everything. It's not like you're a politician's wife."

"Of course I want to come. It's fascinating to hear all of the political ins and outs up close. And it's not as if I have a job at the moment. Everything's at a standstill with Beachcombers until the insurance company finishes its report and cuts us a check."

She forced her eyes to stay dry when more than anything she wanted to shout her frustration over her out-of-control life. She liked simple and uncomplicated.

Matthew Landis was anything and everything except simple and uncomplicated.

His handsome face went somber with concern. "I could always float you a loan—"

"Shut up about the money already." God, he really didn't have a clue about her values and pride in spite of the ring. Still, she eased her words with a smile even as constant reminders of his affluent world whipped by outside in the shape of waterside mansions and high-end cars. "But thank you for the offer. It's very generous of you."

"Don't overrate me. The amount you need wouldn't even put a dent in my portfolio."

She wrinkled her nose and planted her legs firmly on her side of the car—away from his. The leather seats teased at the back of her calves with a reminder of lush accessories she could never afford. "Why did you have to take such a nice offer and downplay it that way?"

"I'm not bragging, only speaking the truth."

That might be so, but it still didn't mean she planned to let him open his wallet to her. Taking money from a man she was sleeping with seemed…icky.

She'd already come too close to crossing a moral conscience line with this fake engagement. She couldn't take one step further. "I see plenty of wealthy people traipsing through Beachcombers who will stiff the waitress on a tip without thinking twice. I know affluence and generosity do not always go hand in hand."

"Since I already have enough debates on my schedule, I won't bother disputing your kind assessment of my character."

She chewed her lip to keep from arguing further and simply listened to the roar and honks of street traffic. The last thing she wanted was to wax on about the wonderful attributes of Matthew Landis. That would do little to bolster her self-control.

He tapped her brow with a warm callused finger. "Penny for them."

She forced a lighthearted smile on her face.

"Come on, surely with your portfolio you can do better than that."

"Touché." He chuckled low, the rumble of his laugh sliding as smoothly over her senses as his arm along the back of the seat to cup her shoulders.

His touch burned along her already heightened nerves, tightening an unwelcome need deep in her belly. She'd always been attracted to him, but the sensual draw was so much more intense now that she knew exactly how high he could nudge her pleasure with even one stroke of his body inside hers.

She inched forward on the seat, her light linen sundress suddenly itchy against her knees. "You don't need to keep up the shows of affection. No one is around to snap a promo shot."

Slowly, torturously so, he slid his arm away, his green eyes glinting with a hint of bad-boy charm that showed he knew exactly how much his touch affected her. "I didn't mean to overstep."

"Apology accepted."

Sheesh, she hated sounding so uptight, but she could barely hold her own with this guy when he *wasn't* touching her. She'd enjoyed having his hands all over her, but she'd hated the way he made her feel the next morning.

"So, what's the going rate for your thoughts?"

"Actually, they're free at the moment." She struggled for some new direction to take their discussion that had nothing to do with touching, needing, wanting. "I'm just not sure if my question is polite."

"I've developed a thick skin over the years."

She wished she could say the same. "All right, then." She tipped her face confidently—and so the vents could shoosh some cooling air against her warming skin. "I can't hush up the accountant in me that's wondering how your family accumulated such a hefty portfolio."

"Dumb luck, as a matter of fact." He scratched his hand along his jaw, which just happened to draw his pointer finger over his top lip in a temptingly seductive manner. "My great-grandfather bought into a big local land deal that paid off well when it just as easily could have tanked."

She remembered clearly how that mouth of his felt exploring every inch of her body, lingering once he discovered a particularly sensitive region. She cleared her throat if not her passion-fogged thoughts. Too easily she could be lured under his sensual spell again and she needed to hold strong. "Uh, where were these land plots?"

"Myrtle Beach." He dropped his hand back to his knee, giving her overloaded senses a momentary reprieve.

"Ah, that explains a lot." Interesting how he downplayed his family's fortune. Wealth that large didn't accumulate on its own or grow by taking care of itself.

"But it doesn't explain everything. Plenty of people blow a fortune before it ever reaches their kids."

"We've invested wisely over the years," he conceded, fingering his cuff links, an antique-looking set that she suspected must have family sentimentality. As she looked closer, she recognized his father's initials. "We've lived well, without question, but always kept an eye on growing the principal."

"Very smart move." Her accounting brain envisioned numerous creative ways to diversify a large holding. Some lucky number cruncher must be having a field day playing with all that capital. "Families expand, so if you don't increase the size of the pie, the pieces will get smaller with each generation."

"Exactly." His thumb polished a rounded cuff link. "We're lucky that we've been able to pursue whatever career dream we wanted without worrying about putting a roof over our heads."

His grass-roots practicality touched her as firmly and stirringly as those callused fingers ever had and that scared her. This man could hurt her, badly, if she wasn't careful.

"It's admirable that you all think that way rather than simply living a life of leisure." The Suburban slowed to a crawl behind cars backed up from a wreck ahead. She forced her drying-up mouth to keep the conversation flowing. "You could simply see the world or something, and nobody would think less of you."

"I could go stark raving nuts, you mean. I like playing golf as much as the next guy—" he gestured at the rolling course packed with players "—but I'm not good enough to make a living at it, therefore it can't be my life's pursuit. For me, politics keeps me in touch with the rest of the world and how they're living. That's a real grounding kind of thing. My brother Kyle says the same about serving in the Air Force."

So this conversation thing wasn't working out as well as she'd expected since he actually got nicer with each sentence. If the traffic jam didn't clear soon she would be in serious trouble. "What about your other brother Sebastian?"

"He's the business lawyer who keeps us all bank-rolled for the next generation."

"And Jonah?"

His smile tightened. "The jury's still out on him."

"He's the youngest, right?" She seemed to recall from the publicity photos of Ginger Landis Renshaw with her boys. "I seem to remember reading he only just graduated from college."

"So did you, but you're not jaunting around the world." He thumbed the crease between his eyebrows. "I'm just not sure how my parents brought up a playboy son."

She followed his words and the mounting proof that there might be something more to him than a fat wallet, a handsome face and slick politician's persona. Definitely dangerous with a warm magnetism that radiated from him and reached to her even when they didn't touch.

"You're a good listener, Ashley."

"You're an interesting speaker." And that was the truth, damn it. Why couldn't he have been a pedantic slug? "I look forward to hearing what you have to say at all those functions. I honestly believe you're the better man for this job and I want to do whatever I can to help make that happen."

"Thank you. You sound like you actually mean that."

She shared a quiet smile with him, unable to miss the enclosed intimacy of just the two of them in the back of the Suburban with a privacy window closed. She started to sway toward him, then jerked her body rigid.

"What's the matter then?" He smoothed a finger along her furrowed forehead much the way he'd smoothed the crease between his own eyebrows.

"I don't have a problem with attending the events with you." She forced her best prim tone in place to put things back on a more practical keel. "My concern is actually more logistical. I don't know how I'm going to get to Charleston and back in time to make everything."

"Who says you have to go back and forth to Charleston?"

Her jaw dropped as her pulse skyrocketed. A fake engagement was one thing. But moving in together? Matthew must have been dipping into the vehicle's liquor cabinet.

Six

Ashley considered availing herself of the Suburban's drink selection after all, time of the afternoon be damned. She could be stuck in here with Matthew for hours if the cops didn't clear the wreck soon.

She tugged at the hem of her dress, because yes, she'd felt his heated gaze stray to her calves more than once during the ride to his house. "You can't be suggesting I should move in with you. The press will chew us up."

"We're engaged." He cupped her elbow.

She shrugged her arm free. She'd been lured by

his sexual draw once before and look where that had landed her? Half dressed on the front page of countless newspapers. "Don't be obtuse and stop touching me."

His eyes narrowed and Ashley mentally kicked herself. Another gauntlet moment.

He slowly removed his hand. "So you're still every bit as attracted to me as I am to you."

Ouch. He played tough.

Well, she would have to meet the challenge. "That line of discussion will not go far in persuading me to stay with you."

One side of his mouth kicked up in a smile. "Point well made." He stretched his arm along the back of the seat, this time without so much as brushing any part of her. "I live in a family compound as do two of my brothers. We all have our own quarters. Mom and the general live in both D.C. and South Carolina. The general's at the Pentagon right now, but Mom's around, so you even have a chaperone."

"By living quarters, what do you mean?" She eyed him warily. He'd made it clear he was still attracted to her and that it wasn't an act. Yet having an affair, with a ring on her finger and the intent to break things off felt wrong. How ironic that she'd been willing to consider sleeping with him when there'd been no jewelry or fake commitments involved. "Is everybody in the same house with a suite, but all still bump into each other walking around in the hall?"

"I thought you objected to me not being around in the morning."

She narrowed her gaze and considered elbowing him in the kidney but that would show he had too much sway over her emotions. "Old issue. No longer relevant."

"Fair enough. Jonah and Sebastian both have suites of rooms in the main house since Jonah graduated and Sebastian's separated from his wife. Kyle has a condo near the Air Force Base in Charleston. And I live in the renovated groundskeeper's carriage house behind the main place. Does that work for you?"

His plan sounded solid and her sister's husband had just arrived home from assignment. While Starr and David would say they didn't mind having her around and they had plenty of space, she had to imagine they would want some privacy. They hadn't been married long and they had the pregnancy news to celebrate. She would be most decidedly a third wheel and it was downright silly to drive back and forth from Charleston to Hilton Head multiple times a day.

Matthew's idea was sensible and bottom line, she was painfully practical.

"Okay and thank you. As long as your brothers

don't run around in their boxer shorts, I guess this should work out all right."

"No worries." Matthew's grin stretched from appealing to downright wicked, sending a shiver of premonition up her spine as the Suburban finally jolted forward. "If I find any of them wearing nothing but their skivvies around you, I'll kick their asses."

Wow, Matthew sure new how to deliver a zinger line to close up shop on conversation. His silence left her with nothing to do but stare out the window.

She'd grown up in Charleston, but this exclusive area of coastal beauty had been meticulously manicured in a way that seemed to preserve yet tame the natural magnificence.

Of course, given the size of the mansions and golf courses they'd passed, the people who lived here could obviously afford to sculpt this place into anything they wished.

The driver steered the SUV along a winding paved drive through palm trees and sea grass until the view parted to reveal a sprawling white three-story house with Victorian peaks overlooking the ocean. A lengthy set of stairs stretched upward to the second story wraparound porch that housed the main entrance. Latticework shielded most of the first floor, which appeared to be a large entertainment area.

Just as in Charleston, many homes so close to the water were built up as a safeguard against tidal floods from hurricanes.

The attached garage had so many doors she stopped counting. His SUV rolled to a stop beside the house, providing a view of the brilliant azaleas behind them and the ocean in front of them. An organic-shaped pool was situated between the house and shore, the waters of the hot tub at the base churning a glistening swirl in the afternoon sun.

"My place is over there." He pointed to the cluster of live oaks and palmettos, a two-story carriage house just visible through the branches.

White with slate-blue shutters, this carriage house was larger than most family homes. She understood he came from money. She had even grown up among wealthy types in Aunt Libby's old Charleston neighborhood. But seeing Matthew's lifestyle laid out so grandly only emphasized their different roots.

She walked up the lengthy stretch of white steps toward the large double doors on the second floor. She gripped the railing and looked out over the water view. "This view. It totally rocks."

He slid an arm around her again. This time she couldn't bring herself to pull away and ruin the moment. She let herself believe she leaned into his embrace simply because they might be seen by someone, the staff, his family.

Had he even told his family the truth? She assumed so but hadn't thought to ask. It was one thing to keep his silence with his campaign manager because as much as you thought you could trust someone, she'd learned it never hurt to be extra careful.

The sound of an opening door plucked her from her reverie. She jerked in Matthew's spicy-scented embrace and turned to find an older woman coming through the main entrance. Even if she hadn't recognized the senator from her press coverage, Ashley would have figured out her identity all the same. Her deep green eyes declared her to be Matthew's mother, even if her fair head contrasted with his dark brown hair.

Ginger Landis Renshaw strode toward them, her shoulder length gray-blond hair perfectly styled. Ashley recalled from news reports the woman was around fifty, but she carried the years well. Wearing a pale pink lightweight sweater set with pearls—and blue jeans—Ginger Landis wasn't at all what Ashley had expected. Thank goodness, because the woman in front of her appeared a little less intimidating.

She had seen the woman often enough on the news—always poised and intelligent, sometimes steely, determined. Today, a softer side showed as she looked at her son then over to Ashley.

"Mother, this is Ashley. Ashley, my mother."

Ginger extended her hands and clasped Ashley's. "Welcome to our home. I'm sorry to hear about what happened to your business, but I'm so glad you're all right and that Matthew brought you here to stay with us."

"Thank you for having me on such short notice, Senator."

"Ginger, please, do call me Ginger."

"Of course," she replied, not yet able to envision herself using the first name of this woman who dined with heads of state.

Matthew's mother studied her, inventory-style, and suddenly Ashley realized the reason for the woman's presence here instead of in D.C. with her husband. Matthew's mother must have been called to give her a Cinderella makeover.

Ashley released Ginger's clasp and crossed her arms over her ill-fitting dress. "It's a pleasure and honor to meet you."

Ginger tipped her head to the side. "Is something wrong, dear?"

Visions blossomed to mind of being stuffed into some stiff sequined gown with her hair plastered in an overdone crafted creation that would make her head ache. She might even be able to pull the look off without appearing to be a joke. She might even look presentable enough to turn a head or two.

But she would feel wretchedly fake and uncomfortable the whole time. "No, of course not. I'm grateful for your generosity in letting me stay here."

"But…?" Ginger prodded.

Ashley let the words tumble free before she could restrain them and end up stuffed in a fashion runway mess. "I just can't help but wonder if Matthew's campaign manager expects you to give me some kind of makeover."

"Why would I want to change you? My son obviously finds you perfect as you are."

"That's very kind of you to say. Thank you." Ashley expected relief only to find something different altogether. She resented the twinge of disappointment sticking inside her chest like an annoying thorn. She truly didn't want some fake redo. She liked herself just fine, but still…

Then another implication of his mother's words soaked in. She didn't appear to know the engagement was fake. That Matthew would keep himself so closed off from even his family gave her pause. Except wasn't she doing the same with her own sisters?

Matthew kissed his mother's cheek. "Always the diplomat." He backed a step. "I'll just go help the driver with our luggage."

Ashley couldn't miss how it didn't seem to dawn on him to allow the chauffeur to haul their suitcases by himself. Yet another touch that made Matthew all the more appealing.

Forcing herself to stop watching him lope down the steps with a muscled grace, she turned her attention to following Ginger back into the house. No mere magazine layout could have done the place justice.

A wall of windows let sunshine stream through and bathe the room in light all the way up to the cathedral ceilings. Hardwood floors were scattered with light Persian rugs around two Queen Anne sofas upholstered in a pale blue fabric with white piping. Wingback chairs in a creamy yellow angled off the side. The whole décor was undoubtedly formal, but in an airy comfortable way.

Ginger spun on her low heel. "I'll show you to your room shortly. The view of the ocean is breathtaking."

Having grown up at Aunt Libby's on the water, she appreciated the sense of home she would get from the sound of the waves lulling her to sleep. Come to think of it, this woman had an Aunt-Libby-like air of kindness to her.

"Your home is gorgeous." Ashley turned to the picturesque windows overlooking the pool and ocean. "Thank you again for letting me stay. I can't wait to unpack my suitcase."

"Oh, my dear, don't worry about doing that. You won't need to use your sister's clothes."

Ashley pivoted away from the windows to the

room filled with the beauty and scent of fresh-cut flowers in crystal vases. "Excuse me, but I thought you said we weren't going to do the makeover deal."

"I never said we weren't going shopping."

"You didn't?" This woman was as good at word-plays and nuances as Matthew. Ashley would have to watch her step around both of them. "What do you mean then?"

"Your entire wardrobe was ruined. It's obvious you need new clothes, even more so because of the predicament with my son and all the appearances you'll need to make together."

"I can't let him pay for my clothes."

Matthew's mother planted her fists on her hips in a stance that brooked no argument. "Since he's the reason you have to attend the functions, it's only fair he pay."

Ashley stayed silent because she knew she wouldn't win a war of words with this master stateswoman.

Ginger smiled. "Prideful. I like you more and more by the minute." She waved a manicured hand. "I wasn't born into all of this. I didn't even know about it when I met my first husband, an Air Force jet-jock who swept me off my feet so much we eloped in two weeks."

A sweet-sad smile flickered across her face as the

soft sounds of someone turning on a vacuum in the next room filled the silence.

Ashley touched her arm. "How long has he been gone?"

"Nearly eleven years. I never thought I would fall in love that way again. And in a sense, I was right. Love built slower for me the second time around, but no less strong."

Ginger's eyes took on a faraway look and Ashley realized the woman was staring at an old family photo across the room for at least half a minute before she returned her attention back to the present. "So, Ashley, about the shopping spree. I adore the general and my boys, but there are times I need a girls' day out."

Wow, this lady had a way of working a person around to her side of the argument. "How about this? He can pay for the clothes I use at official functions, but I pay for anything else I wear."

"That sounds entirely fair and wonderfully honorable."

"Matthew's campaign manager says the media will eat me alive."

Ginger cupped her cheek, her charm bracelet jingling. "No one expects you to change who you are. We're only here to help you be comfortable as *yourself.* We'll be doing that with new clothes of your choosing and some helpful tips for dealing with the press."

Ah man, she really didn't want to like this woman so much. Forming any kind of bond with Matthew's family would only make things all the tougher when she walked away.

At least she could take some comfort in the sincerity lacing Ginger's words. Matthew's mother would help her choose appropriate clothes that stayed true to her own tastes.

There wouldn't be a Cinderella makeover after all. Which was a relief. Except that as much as she knew she and Matthew weren't right for each other long-term, a part of her wouldn't have minded knocking him flat on his awesome butt.

He was only just finishing up his first speech of the day and already he was sweating—big-time.

Except he couldn't blame the crowd or the press or even the cranking summer heat. His pumping blood pressure had more to do with the demure woman sitting serenely to his right in his peripheral vision, her attention unwaveringly focused on him.

The way Ashley's sheathe dress kept hitching up over her knees was about to send him into cardiac arrest at thirty years old. His mother had absconded with Ashley yesterday afternoon, not returning until well after supper. Call him crazy, but he'd been expecting pastel suits and pearls like his mother wore.

Instead, his mother had picked an emerald-green form-fitting dress with a scooped neck and a pendant that drew his gaze south. A daring choice given all he'd heard about everyone appearing subdued during a campaign. Yet Ashley, with her long auburn hair pulled back with a simple gold clasp, looked classically elegant. The no-heel strappy sandals accented with gold stones matching the necklace flashed a tribute to her glowing youthfulness. She would easily appeal to a cross section of voters.

She easily appealed to *him* at a time when he'd sworn he would keep his distance.

He resisted the urge to swipe his wrist over his brow, a dead giveaway to anyone with a camera that he was rattled. He glanced quickly at his notes to scoop up his ender. Thank God he must have said something coherent because everyone clapped and smiled.

The Rotary president stepped up to the microphone to invite questions from the media.

An older woman stood, her press pass around her neck tangled in the buttons of her tan sweater. "Miss Carson, tell us how Congressman Landis proposed? Was it before or after the revealing photos of the two of you hit the papers?"

Yeah, that had lots to do with the issues.

His campaign manager on his left shot to his feet. "Come on, Mary." Brent smiled at the seasoned reporter. "You know Ashley's still new to all of this. How about you don't put the screws to her just yet?"

Ashley placed a soft hand on Matthew's arm, gently nudging him from the podium. "It's all right. I would like to answer."

Matthew heard his campaign manager suck in air faster than a dehydrated person gulped down water. Matthew worried more than a little himself, but he wouldn't embarrass Ashley by silencing her. He would simply stand by in case she threw him a panicked "save me" look.

"As you can tell, Matthew has concerns for me and the stresses of campaign scrutiny. That's why he tried to keep me out of the limelight. So I solved the problem by proposing to him."

Chuckles rumbled through the crowd while reporters went wild taking notes. He had to admit, she'd handled the question well while sticking to the truth.

She cast a shy glance through her eyelashes. "You'll have to pardon me if I insist the rest of the details are *very* personal and private." The laughter swelled again. Ashley waited patiently for the hubbub to subside. "And I know when to end on a positive note. Thank you for having us here today."

Matthew palmed the small of her back and ushered her toward the exit behind the podium. The door swooshed behind them, muffling clicking cameras. He leaned and captured her lips with his—hey, wait, where had that idea come from?—but too late, he'd already done it. He was totally entranced with the way she'd glowed behind that podium. So much so, all his good intentions for protecting her with distance had flown right the hell out the window.

Now that he had her against him again, the taste of her fresh on his tongue, he had to savor the moment for an extra stroke longer before easing the kiss to an end. He settled her against his chest instead while he regained control.

"You did a fantastic job handling that reporter, Ashley."

"I answered truthfully." Her fingers gripped his lapels, her words breathy in the narrow corridor leading to a brightly lit Exit sign out of the small community college auditorium.

"You answered artfully." He forced himself to step back, but couldn't bring himself to release her arms, convenient since she still held his jacket. "There's a skill to that."

"It was worth it to hear your campaign manager go on life support."

"I was hoping you wouldn't notice."

"He has no reason to trust me. I don't have a track record." Her eyebrows pinched together. "Matthew, I've been waiting for the right time to ask you something, but there are always people around, so I may as well spill it now. Why haven't you told your family the truth?"

"Why haven't you?"

"Answering a question with a question isn't going to work this time."

He gave her the truth as best he understood it. "So much of my life is an open book. I prefer to keep things private when I can." As he'd done about his relationship with Dana. Ashley had a way of pushing his buttons and making him open up before he realized it, a decidedly uncomfortable feeling. "Besides, my family would only worry if they knew, which I suspect is the same reason you haven't told your sisters."

"You're very perceptive." She relaxed against his chest, soft, sweet smelling and too sexy given the way she'd been turning him inside out all morning long.

"I'm sorry you're in this position at all." And damn but he knew to be more careful in his word choices. Now the word positions had him thinking of all the different ways he would like to have Ashley under him, over him, around him. "If I could go back and do things differently, I—"

He stopped. He couldn't complete the sentence because he realized without question that he wouldn't give up that night with Ashley, even realizing how things would turn out. God, but that made him a selfish bastard.

Her eyes locked with his, her lips parting slightly. She arched up on her toes just as he felt his head magnetically drawn back down toward her. His mouth grazed hers, once, twice, only long enough for a gentle nip that sent his insides aching for more. What harm could there be in exploring the sexual side of things? A brief affair... More of the taste of Ashley...

The door swung open, cutting short the moment if not his desire. His campaign manager barged toward them, not bothering to slam the door, damn him, undoubtedly more than happy for the reporters to snap a shot now.

Brent clapped his hands together. "Okay, lovebirds, time to get this show on the road."

Matthew watched Ashley as she followed Brent out the door. He didn't want a committed relationship and he most definitely was not giving his heart away again. However, something told him as he watched Ashley, new confidence swinging in her step, he might not be able to walk away as easily as he'd imagined.

Seven

Enjoying the play of moonlight across the ocean, Ashley gripped the railing of the harbor cruise paddle boat as it docked and thought of the thousand questions she'd answered since yesterday morning. Hands she'd shaken. Babies she'd cradled.

The last part had been the easiest because those little constituents didn't vote. She hadn't realized until the morning paper that she'd been lured into the most cliché campaign moment possible. Thinking about her every move and word was downright exhausting, especially when she and Matthew actually knew so little about each other. She really should make out a questionnaire asking about funky facts from his past.

Tonight had been pleasant with the romantic setting and fairly tasty meal—Beachcombers could have provided better, of course—but the evening had been nice. Except for the fact she'd barely seen Matthew. She rubbed her arms, trying to will away the irritation she had no right to experience. She focused instead on the beauty around her.

Lights were strung along the paddle boat cruiser. Dinner tables were littered along one deck. The upper deck rang with swing-band dance music. A waiter strolled by with a silver platter resting on one palm, perfectly balancing the tray of champagne flutes.

Matthew stepped from the shadows, sipping his seltzer water. His eyes scanned down with obvious approval glinting and she winged a prayer of thanks to Ginger Landis Renshaw, her fairy godmother who'd been wise enough not to try to transform her into Cinderella. Instead, she'd simply helped Ashley fine tune her own tastes in ways she never could have envisioned on her own.

She certainly wouldn't have thought to select a dress that left her shoulders bare. She'd always tried to cover the uneven tilt with layers—the more the better. But then Ginger had pulled out the simple cream dress stitched in gold with a plunging V-neck in the front and back. She'd dreamed of this sort of satiny fabric sliding over her skin. Ginger had added a lightweight, gold shawl.

Matthew tipped back his water glass and drained the whole thing as if his throat were parched.

Ashley savored the moment and searched for small talk to keep him standing with her. "You're not drinking any of that top-notch champagne?"

"Seems like a recipe for disaster, mixing alcohol and reporters." He glanced at Ashley's drink.

She rattled her ice, saddened again that they knew so little about each other. "Seltzer water for me, too, but with a lime."

"My apologies for jumping to conclusions. Let me get you a refill to make up for ignoring you all evening."

"Thank you." Most of all for noticing that she'd been left to her own devices. That eased the sting.

She leaned back against the rail, studying the couples dancing up on the deck. The ocean wind carried snippets of conversations her way from partiers as well as people milling about and disembarking down the gangplank. She paid little attention until her ear snagged on a familiar voice, the campaign manager's brisk baritone.

"She did better than I expected."

"That's not saying much," another man responded, a voice she vaguely recognized from a telephone briefing she'd received earlier. "Your expectations weren't very high."

"Well, what can I say?" Brent answered. "She wasn't what I would have chosen for him on the campaign trail or as a senator's wife. She brings nothing to the table politically except that shy little smile. However, what's done is done. He will have to make the best of things. At least she won't outshine him."

Ouch. That one hurt more than a little. But then eavesdroppers rarely heard good about themselves.

"I thought Ginger did a decent job with the makeover," the other man continued, "not too flashy, not too schoolmarmish. The outfit is classy but Ashley doesn't look like someone playing dress-up with her mother's clothes."

"Yeah, about that age thing. What the hell was Matthew thinking? She's only what, twenty-four? The pressure is going to demolish her."

Ashley had heard enough. She refused to stand around like an insecure wimp, regardless of how much their words hurt, reminding her yet again how she was the wrong kind of woman for Matthew. At least she could make sure they never knew how deeply the barbs dug.

She stepped out of the shadows. "Twenty-*three*, thank you very much. I am twenty-three. You of all people should have your facts in order better than that. But thanks for the extra year of maturity vote of confidence to go along with my honors diploma in accounting from the College of Charleston."

"Ah hell." Brent had the good grace to wince while music echoed on the sea breeze. "We didn't see you there. I'm sorry for speaking out of turn in a public setting."

"Apology accepted." There was no use in making an enemy of the man. She just didn't want his pity because it played on her already pervasive sense that she couldn't be the kind of woman Matthew needed. "Although I would warn you of a very good piece of advice I received at a briefing recently. Never, *never* speak a sound bite you wouldn't want repeated."

"Point well taken," the campaign manager agreed, hesitating only long enough to check for privacy. "But hear me on this. I've been around this business a long time and you're not cut out for this. Most importantly, Martin Stewart is a wily opponent not to be taken lightly and you're not helping Matthew."

Before Ashley could answer, Matthew rounded the corner with her drink in hand. "Here you are, Ashley. I thought I'd lost you to another reporter." He passed the glass to her. "Your sparkling water, complete with a twist of lime."

"Thank you." The tart taste fit right in with her souring mood.

Matthew's eyes narrowed. "Is everything all right here?"

Ashley stirred her drink with the thin straw, unwilling to risk causing any scene or rift between Matthew and his campaign manager.

She stabbed her straw through the ice. "Everything's fine. Why shouldn't it be? Your manager is just discussing ways I can be more helpful on the campaign trail."

Matthew slid an arm around her waist. "She doesn't have to do anything other than be herself."

Ashley appreciated him saying that, but she knew full well she hadn't offered anything substantive to his campaign beyond stopping rumors he was indiscriminately sleeping around.

Brent leaned back on the rail on both elbows. "I worry about the two of you."

"Just do your job." Matthew's voice took on that renowned Landis icy tone. "If you have anything more to say on this subject, we can take it up at headquarters later."

"You're the boss." Brent shoved away from the rail and walked away with his companion.

Matthew narrowed his eyes at the retreating man, then turned back to Ashley. "Did he say something to upset you?"

"Nothing. Really. Everything's fine."

Matthew brushed a thumb over her cheekbone,

glancing around much like Brent when he'd checked to be sure no one could overhear. "You look tired. You've got dark circles under your eyes."

His words, too close to Brent's concerns, pissed her off when her emotions were already raw. She wasn't a weakling, damn it. "What a smooth talker you are."

"Beautiful—but tired. I realize campaigning can be a grind." He stepped away, taking her drink from her and placing it on a deck table alongside his. "We're leaving now."

"You can't go." She looked around at the people still dancing on the upper deck. "This is your party."

"I most certainly can punch out whenever I want. We've docked. Others are disembarking. I learned a while back if I stay 'til lights out at every function I'm on hand when the party turns wild and that never goes well for a politician come picture time."

When he put it that way…. She tucked her hand in the crook of his elbow. "Well, by all means then, let's blow this pop stand before Mrs. Hamilton-Reis hangs her bra in place of the flag."

Chuckling, he shuddered. "Thanks for placing that image in my mind."

"Always happy to please."

His eyes narrowed. "You do please me, you know. Very much, Ashley Carson." He dipped his head and brushed his mouth along her ear. "I'm so very sorry

I messed things up for the chance to please *you* again."

His words sent a thrill of excitement and power up her spine. Sure, Brent Davis's years of political wisdom attested to reasons she wasn't the wisest choice to stand by Matthew's side, at least for tonight, she could have one more memory to tuck away.

And she intended to make the most of it.

Strolling along the private shoreline outside his home with Ashley, Matthew wondered if he'd pushed too hard too fast by saying something suggestive to Ashley on the boat. He wanted an affair with her, but he already sensed they wouldn't have much time. She would cut and run from his lifestyle soon enough, without a doubt.

But all the touching and kissing for the camera was playing hell with his libido. He'd suggested this barefoot walk alone along the shore to cool them both down before they turned in for the night. A long night. Likely alone, because as much as he wanted her, she would have to set the pace this time.

Ashley kicked her way through the rolling surf, her gold shawl billowing behind her in the breeze. Creamy white fabric with its tantalizing glimmers of gold stitching molded to her chest the way he wanted to fit his palms against her curves.

Gathering the hem of her gown up to her knees, she shot ahead a couple of paces before spinning on her bare feet to face him, her loose hair streaking around her face. "What did you dress up as for Halloween as a kid?"

Her question blindsided him more than anything he'd heard from the most seasoned reporter. Of course that could also have something to do with his lust-fogged brain at the moment. "Excuse me? I'm accustomed to obscure questions from the press, but that one came way out of left field."

"Then I guess it's an excellent question." Her gentle laugh carried on the salty breeze as light as any meringue, simple, but damn fine. "It just struck me over the past couple of days that we really don't know that much about each other. Those holes in our knowledge could be a real pitfall in an interview. So? What about your childhood holidays?"

He thought back to all those pictures in his mother's countless family photo albums. "A cop. I trick-or-treated as a cop."

"And?"

Matthew shook his head, his shoes dangling from his fingers. Water slapped at the dock where the family speedboat bucked with each wave. "Always a policeman for Halloween. Drove my mom nuts. She really got into making us new costumes each year and I kept asking for the same one, just in a bigger size."

"If you wanted to be a police officer, what made you want to go into politics?"

"Who said I wanted to be a cop as an adult? Just because I dressed up like one as a kid doesn't mean…" He scratched his head. "Okay, never mind. Fair question. Politics is the family business. It's only natural I would follow this path."

"Your father was in the Air Force before becoming a senator." She scraped her hair back from her face. "And your brothers chose different paths."

"That they did." He thought back to their childhood years, putting on costumes in preparation for the day they would be able to play out their dreams for real. "We're looking for ways to serve our country."

"You could have done that on the police force."

"My father died."

She slowed to fall in pace alongside him. Not touching, just there. More present in the moment than most people who got right up in somebody's face. "That must have been an awful time for you."

"He didn't get to complete his term." There was something so damn sad about unfinished business— his father's term, his old fiancée's diploma never picked up.

An engagement never fulfilled with vows.

"Your mother served out his term, and very well I might add. Life has a way of working things out, even the bad things, given time."

"You're right." He needed to remember that more often and concentrate on his own reasons for taking on this office rather than doing it for anyone else. Interesting how Ashley focused him with a few words.

And hell, what was he doing selfishly spilling his guts when he was standing under the stars with a beautiful woman? She turned attention to others so artfully he wondered how many missed the chance to uncover fascinating things about her.

He tipped her chin. "What about you?"

"What about me what?"

"Your Halloween costumes." He walked alongside her, smiling down and trying to envision her as a kid, probably skinny with hair that weighed more than she did. And a heart bigger than all of that combined. "What did you pick, and I want a list."

"A pirate, a zebra, a hobo, a ninja, Cleopatra— the fake snake was tons of fun." She clicked off the years on her fingers. "A doctor, oh, and once I was a pack of French fries. Starr was a hot dog and Claire insisted she was a gourmet quiche, but we all knew it was a pecan pie with fake bacon bits sewn on."

"Wow, your foster mom organized that for all her kids?" Did Ashley realize she was walking closer to him?

Her arm skimmed his.

Her leg brushed his with every step.

Was she trying to seduce him, for God's sake?

"Aunt Libby had this huge box full of old costumes and clothes. She was constantly adding items to it throughout the year—picking up additions on clearance or from yard sales." She looked up at him, her brown eyes the perfect backdrop to reflect the stars overhead. "Actually, we didn't only use it for Halloween. We played dress-up year round."

"I'd enjoy seeing pictures of that."

Her smile faded. "If they survived the fire."

He slid an arm around her shoulders and tucked her to his side, holding her closer when she didn't object. "Tell me more about the dress-up games."

"We made quite a theatrical troop with our play acting. We could be anything, say anything and leave the world behind once those costumes were in place. Looking back, I can see how she must have been using some play therapy for a group of wounded girls."

"She sounds like an amazing lady."

"She was. I miss her a lot." Ashley stared up at him with far-too-insightful starlit eyes. "The way you must miss your father."

He tried to clear his throat but the lump swelled to fist-size and wouldn't dislodge.

Ashley slipped her arm under his jacket and around his waist. "That's why you're in politics then, to feel closer to him?"

Her touch seemed to deflate the lump and he found himself able to push words free again. "That's why I started, yes, and then I found out along the way why it was so important to him. It's not about power. And sure the chance to make a difference at a grass-roots level is…mind-blowing. But there's more to it."

"And that would be?"

"Honestly, this has gotten to be such a dirty business no sane person would even want to enter a race. Between the sound-bite hungry press and cut-throat opponents, no one can possibly lead a life clean or perfect enough to undergo that level of scrutiny. There will be blood in the water at some point and sharks will circle."

"Okay, you're really depressing me here, so how about getting to the point soon."

He chuckled low, the crash of waves stealing the sand from under his feet. "Right. Gotta work on paring down my stump-speech skills. My point? I can't let fear keep me out of the race."

"Good people have to step up to the plate, too."

"Thanks." He gave her a one-armed hug.

"For what?"

"For calling me 'good people.'" And damned if that simple hug hadn't pressed her breast against his side, which had him thinking decidedly un-good-guy thoughts about seducing her right here. Right now. Behind the nearest sand dune.

She stopped, dropping her shoes onto the sand,

then taking his and tossing them aside, as well. She clasped both of his hands in hers. "You've been worried about our engagement fib."

He stayed silent for three swooshes of the waves.

She squeezed his fingers. "Doing the wrong thing for all the right reasons is tough to reconcile. I know. I've been wrestling with the same issue."

"What conclusion did you arrive at?"

"Good people are also fallible humans. Sometimes we deserve a break, even if it's only a temporary reprieve."

He skimmed his knuckles over the ivory clear and soft skin of her face, over her chin, down her neck. She gazed up at him, her eyes so deep and darkening as her pupils expanded.

If he let himself, he could fall…right…in.

He kissed her. He had to. The past couple of days they'd been dancing around this moment and he knew the solid reasons why he should wait to pursue the attraction, give her time, romance her more. But here, tonight, under the stars, he wanted her and he could feel that she wanted him, too, from the way she wriggled to get closer. He couldn't sense even the least bit of hesitation in her response.

Her breathy sigh into his mouth reminded him of other times she'd gasped out her pleasure. This usually shy woman certainly tossed away her inhibitions when it came to the sensual.

She gripped his lapels, her fists tugging tighter, pulling him closer as she pressed herself to him. Her lips parted, her tongue meeting his every bit as aggressively as he sought hers. She tasted of citrus from her lime water earlier, more potent than any alcohol. Her soft breasts molded temptingly against his chest and his hands itched to stroke her without the barrier of clothes or possible interruption.

As much as he ached to have her here, out in the open with the sky and waves all around them, he knew that wasn't practical. "We should take this inside before we lose control."

"And before someone with a telephoto lens gets an up-close and personal of the total you."

"Not an image I want recorded for posterity."

Laughing, she clasped his hand and dashed toward his white clapboard carriage house. She kept the hem of her dress hitched in one fist, a mesmerizing dichotomy in her formal gown and bare feet.

Matthew tugged at her hand. "Our shoes."

She smiled back at him, her eyes full of total desire. "To hell with our shoes."

Staring back at her, he knew he wouldn't say no to Ashley in full tilt temptress mode. He just wished he could be sure his conscience would fare better against the harsh morning light than their shoes would against the elements.

Eight

Ashley gripped Matthew's hand as he led her past sprawling oak trees to his two-story carriage house. The quaint white home with gray-blue shutters gleamed like a beacon with the security lights strategically placed. Sand clung to her skin, rasping along her hyper-revved nerves as she raced by fragrant azaleas up the stone steps after him.

He swung the gray door wide and hauled her into the pitch dark hallway. Before she could blink, he'd slammed the door closed and pressed her against the wood panel for a kiss that sent her blood crashing through her veins like out-of-control waves during a hurricane. His hands were planted on either side of her head as he seduced her with nothing more than his mouth on hers. The taste of lingering ocean spray mingled with the lemon from his water earlier. Her shawl shimmered down her arms to pool around her feet.

Her foot stroked along the back of his calf, her sandy feet rasping against the fine fabric of his trousers. She grasped at his back, stroking and gripping and stroking more, lower, urging him closer until his body sealed flush against hers. And oh yes, she could feel how much he wanted her, too. She rocked against the hard length of him, searching, aching for release.

Matthew tore his mouth from hers and nipped along her jaw until he reached her ear where he buried his face in her hair, his five-o'clock shadow gently abrading her skin. Her eyes adjusting to the dark, she could see the straining tendons in his neck. His breath flamed over her in hot bursts.

"Ashley, we need to slow this down a notch if I'm going to make it to the bedroom, or at least to the sofa."

She didn't want to stop, even for the short stretch of hardwood it would take to reach the leather couch a few feet away in the moonlit living room. "Why move then? As long as you've got protection in your pocket, I'm more than happy with right here, right now."

His low growl of approval sent a shiver of excitement up her spine.

He tugged his wallet free. "I've been carrying protection since that first night with you. I knew full well the chemistry between us could combust again without warning."

Matthew plucked out a condom and pitched his wallet over his shoulder. The thud of leather against wood snapped what little restraint she had left.

In a flurry of motion she barely registered since he'd started kissing her again, she grappled with his belt while he bunched the hem of her clingy cream dress in his fists, higher, higher still until he reached her waist. With one impatient hand he gripped the thin scrap of her satin panties—and how she delighted in the fact that when she'd shopped for underwear, she hadn't selected so much as a single piece of practical cotton.

She managed to open his fly and encircle him with a languorous glide of her fingers along his hot hard arousal. His jaw flexed. His grip twisted on her panties until they…snapped.

Cool air swooshed along her overheated flesh in an excruciating contrast. "Now," she gasped against his mouth. "To hell with foreplay."

"If you insist," he groaned between gritted teeth.

She couldn't resist watching every intimate detail as he rolled the sheathe into place. Matthew hitched an arm under her bottom and lifted her against the door until the heat of him nudged perfectly between her legs. Inch by delicious inch, he lowered her as he filled her. She hooked her legs around his waist and pressed him the rest of the way home.

Tremors began quaking through her before he even moved and she realized their every touch in the days prior had been foreplay leading to this. He eased away. Then thrust into her with a thick abandon that sent her over the edge without warning.

Her head flung back against the door as she cried out with each wave cresting through her. Her heels dug deeper into his buttocks. Matthew moved faster, taking the waves higher. His shout of completion spurred a final wash of pleasure, and her body went limp.

They stood locked together silently for…well, she wasn't sure how long. Then he released her and her feet slid to the floor. She started to sag, her muscles too weak with satisfaction to hold her, and he scooped her into his arms.

"I've got you, Ashley. Just relax."

She hummed her approval against his chest. She would figure out how to talk again later.

On his way through the small foyer, he paused for her to flick one of the light switches, bathing the room in a low glow. As he strode into the living room, she lounged sated against his chest and took a moment to learn more about Matthew from his surroundings. Deep burgundy leather chairs and a sofa filled the airy room, angled for a perfect view of both the ocean and the wide-screened television. Striped wool hooked rugs scattered along tile into an open-area dining room and high-tech kitchen.

And dead center across the room—a narrow hallway that undoubtedly led to the bedrooms.

He stopped beside the sofa. "Do you want to stay here or head back there?"

"There, please." She wanted to learn more about him beyond his political standings, affinity for leather furniture and childhood love of cop costumes.

"Lucky for me, that's exactly where I want to be, too. Actually, anywhere you are without your clothes sounds perfect to me."

Even as she told herself to savor the sensations of the here and now, she couldn't help fearing the out-of-control waves of emotion Matthew stirred could drown her in the end. If so, tonight would be all she could afford to risk.

This could all be simpler than he'd predicted.

Matthew carried Ashley back toward his bed-room, wondering if he'd overthought this whole situation. They got along well and the chemistry hadn't been a one-time fluke. Why not ride the wave? Friendship with rocking hot sex could be an awesome, uncomplicated alternative to spending the rest of their lives alone or locked in some relationship where emotions ruled their lives to the exclusion of all else.

He grazed a quick kiss along her passion-swollen lips before easing her onto his bed. Yeah, he liked the look of her there. And he would enjoy it even more once he peeled her clothes from her sweet body.

Apparently Ashley had the same idea, because she arched up from the bed to kiss him with an ardent intent that made it clear she was ready for round two. He draped his jacket over the chair without ever breaking contact with her mouth. She tugged his tie with frantic fingers, loosening until finally the length slid free from his collar. She flicked the silk over her shoulder and set to work on the buttons down the front of his shirt until she glided her cool finger inside along his bare skin.

Matthew kissed aside one shoulder strap of her dress. With the dress's built in bra and her panties out on the foyer floor, she was perilously close to total exposure.

He smiled in anticipation against her flowery scented skin. "At least we're going to make it to a bed this time."

She shoved his pants down and away. He kicked them to the side. "I liked the hall."

"Me, too." He liked *her* anywhere. "But this time we're going to take it slower."

Matthew brushed away and down both straps of her gown, guiding it over her breasts, teasing along her hips until it slithered to her feet. He couldn't resist stilling for a moment to take her in. It seemed like longer than a handful of days since he'd had the pleasure of seeing her naked.

He remembered her being hot. He dreamed of her sexiness. But he'd forgotten or hadn't taken the time to notice some of the more intimate details of her body—such as the enticing mole on her hip that he now traced with his thumb to better imprint it in his memory. Countless other nuances of Ashley burned themselves into his brain.

Then she flattened her hand to his chest and brought a close to his ability to think. Time to feel. To touch. He traced her collarbone with his tongue, working kisses and nips lower to her tempting curves until his mouth closed over the peak of one breast, drawing it tighter, then shifting his attention to the other equally sweet swell, in need of more, more of her, sooner than he'd expected after their mind-blowing encounter in the hall. She arched against him and then they were both tumbling onto the bed.

She slid her hands down his back and cupped his taut buttocks, digging in her fingers, urging him closer. "Now, Matthew."

He clasped her wrists and gently eased them to the side. "Slower this time, remember?"

"Forget about slower. We have all flipping night for slower." She wriggled temptingly under him.

He trailed kisses between her breasts, shifting his hold on her wrists to link fingers with her. He nipped along her rib cage, working his way south.

He blew air against her stomach, lower, lower still until she gasped.

"Matthew?"

"FTW," he mumbled against her.

"What?"

He glanced up the length of her creamy white body and grinned. "FTW. For the win, lady. I'm going for the win."

Ashley swept her hand through the frothy hot tub waters, reclining back into the warmth of Matthew's naked strength serving as the perfect "arm chair." His Jacuzzi was built into the bathroom with a skylight overhead, which offered the aura of being outside without the loss of privacy.

After making love again in his bedroom, he'd shown her the oversize bathroom that had been an add-on to the carriage house. Just as she'd sunk into the full tub, he'd returned with champagne and strawberries—and joined her. The added bulk of his body eased the water just over the tips of her breasts, the gentle swoosh a warm temptation.

As much as she wanted to relax into the moment,

sipping her drink, enjoying the burst of fruit on her taste buds as Matthew fed her, her stomach kept tightening with nerves. Things with Matthew were getting more complicated by the second.

Damn it, she should be happy. She'd fantasized over what it would be like with this man. He wasn't hotfooting toward the door like after their first night together. So why did his ring suddenly feel so utterly heavy on her finger?

Matthew's hands landed on her shoulders and he began a soothing massage. "I'm sorry you're so tense. I hate to think this campaign put those kinks in your muscles."

"I'm managing." She sipped from the fluted crystal, the fine vintage tickling her nose as surely as the bristly hair on Matthew's chest teased her back.

"You're more than managing." He rested his chin on her head while continuing to knead her kinked muscles. "But you don't care for the spotlight?"

Just what she needed, reminders of Brent Davis's concerns that she could actually hurt Matthew's chances of beating that Martin Stewart. She stayed silent, finishing her drink and splaying her fingers through the rose-scented bubbles.

Steam saturated her senses. The mirror may have fogged a while ago, but she still carried in her memory the reflected image of the two of them together in the gray-and-white marble tub.

His firm caress continued its seductive magic. "Not much longer and hopefully things will settle out."

She couldn't imagine how. Every scenario that played out in her mind—continuing this charade or walking away—spelled frustration.

Perhaps her best solution would be to avoid the whole subject altogether tonight and focus on the sensations of the here and now. "That feels amazing."

His thumbs worked their way up her neck. "This Jacuzzi has eased a lot of tense muscles after working out with my brothers."

"I was talking about your hands, but yeah, the hot tub is awesome, too."

He circled the pressure points along her jaw. "I'm glad to hear you like my touch."

"Very much." Too much. This had been easier when he'd been the unattainable fantasy of a woman convinced he would never look twice at her.

She tapped her left shoulder, the one still slightly raised and blurted, "I had scoliosis as a girl."

His massaging fingers tensed for a second, an understated indication he had heard her.

"I'm lucky Aunt Libby aggressively addressed the problem with my spine early." She knew that now, although she'd hated the brace as a child. "For the most part it doesn't affect the way I live anymore. Although I shy away from higher heels and standing for too long without moving can give me a headache."

"Well, as I understand it, mega-high heels aren't good for anybody's back and standing still for an hour is highly overrated."

His easy acceptance of the subject released more tension inside her than the massaging tub jets ever could. "No way did I just hear what I thought I heard."

"What did I say?"

"A man actually dissed high heels for women?" She glanced over her shoulder and crinkled her nose at him. "No freaking way. I thought the whole male species stopped for a woman's legs extended by spike heels."

He cocked one eyebrow at her. "How un-PC of you. You make us sound very shallow."

"You said it. Not me."

"Ouch. Low blow, but well played. Perhaps you should stand in for me during the debates." He slipped his arms around her, just below her breasts. "Certainly everybody has physical traits that they're attracted to."

"Like legs?"

His hands slid up to cup her, his thumbs brushing against her nipples. "Or breasts." His head dipped to her ear. "Or the soft feel of your skin." He nuzzled her neck. "And there's your amazing hair."

"You're quite a smooth talker."

"I'm only being honest." His hands stilled again, clasped over her stomach. "Why do you have such trouble accepting compliments?"

He'd been so understanding about the subject thus far, she allowed herself the risk of sharing more about the other hurts, the emotional kind, that the birth defect had brought her over the years. "Left-over issues from the scoliosis I imagine."

"You're blessedly healthy." His eyes blazed with an unmistakable intensity and reminder of how much worse things could have been.

"Yes, and I'm grateful for the amazing doctors who helped me over the years." She hesitated. "But you didn't see me before. Achieving this posture wasn't easy. Some people—my biological parents— didn't want the financial and time-consuming strain I brought."

Matthew's muscles turned to Sheetrock against her back. She looked over her shoulder to find his eyes were equally as hard.

"They didn't deserve you." His words were gentle, but his body still rigid.

With indignation. Fury even. She read it all there in his eyes so gemstone sharp they could cut. He was angry *for her.* People had been sympathetic, helpful, but she couldn't recall anyone being flat-out mad for that ill-treated little girl she'd been.

Matthew touched her soul and wiped away years of pain. "Thank you."

"No need to thank me, I'm just stating a fact." He held her gaze. "And while I'm on the subject, you're undoubtedly a tough lady."

That felt good to hear, as well, especially after Brent's scathing assessment of her character.

"I had to be. Children can be cruel to a kid who doesn't look like the rest of them." Even adults— her biological parents—could be horribly unaccepting of their daughter's twisted gait.

Matthew was right. They hadn't deserved her. How mind-blowing that she'd never before considered that they simply weren't cut out for parenthood.

Muscles she hadn't even realized were still tensed eased at the new level of understanding. She'd talked about this with Aunt Libby and her sisters often over the years. Interesting—and a bit scary—that it had taken just one conversation with this man to help her see things with a different perspective.

Matthew skimmed a knuckle down her spine. "You wore a brace all the time?"

"Until college, then I only had to wear it at night." She cast another quick glance over her shoulder. "That's why I'm so addicted to silky fabrics now. They feel all the more fabulous on my skin."

"You're obviously a sensualist." His hands glided back around her with a touch as light as any fabric.

"I'm an accountant."

"So? People who like numbers can't like sensations and even adventurous sex?"

"When you put it that way…" And touched her that way.

"You're perfect the way you are." His thumbs grazed the undersides of her breasts while he dipped his head to tease along her collarbone. "All of that in the past made you into the sexy, smart woman you are today."

His arousal throbbed an agreement against the base of her spine. She slid her hands under the churning water to caress his powerful legs, wriggling in his lap, her pulse already pounding in her ears as loudly as the blasts of water through the Jacuzzi jets.

He cupped her waist and lifted her slightly, urging her to turn around until she knelt, her damp legs on either side of his. She leaned forward until the core of her pressed to the hard and ready length of him. Her breasts teased his chest as she leaned forward to capture a kiss.

Tonight wasn't over yet and she was determined to make the most of it.

She arched up until the heat of him nestled against her, then she slid down, slowly taking him inside her, tantalizingly so, torturously so. "FTW, Matthew. For the win."

Nine

"FTW, brother."

His brother's ill-chosen words echoing in his ears, Matthew choked midway through his golf swing and shanked the ball into a water hazard near the clubhouse. Wading birds swooped upward and out of the way.

Matthew scowled over his shoulder at his middle brother who knew the no-speaking rule. "Thanks, Sebastian."

He'd been looking forward to this afternoon of golf with his brothers, even if the event also happened to be a benefit tournament. However, if he kept playing like this, the foursome on the fairway behind them would have to stop for lunch before they could move ahead.

"No problem, bro. Always happy to cheer you on." Their lawyer sibling did have impeccable timing. "Nice slice, by the way."

The other two Landis brothers stood by the golf cart applauding with grins as smug as the one on the gator's face as the reptile slid through the salt marsh. Nope, not gonna wade in after that ball. He would take the drop for a penalty stroke.

Matthew pointed his titanium driver at the youngest, Jonah, first and then at Kyle, the next to oldest. "Your turns are coming up soon enough, and I feel a coughing fit coming on."

They'd all grown up competing with each other and nothing had changed now. He couldn't fault them for it, and of course Sebastian had no way of knowing just what a kick in the gut his FTW would apply. He and Ashley had both won in a major way throughout the night.

Matthew reached into the tiny trash can on the side of his cart and scooped out a handful of the grass seed mixed with sand. He leaned down to pack it into the divot he'd chunked out of the course when his swing had gone awry.

Thoughts of Ashley tended to send his brain off-kilter in much the same manner. He leaned on his club, images of her facing him in the hot tub threatening what little concentration he had left. They hadn't gotten much sleep, but he wouldn't change a minute of their night together.

He glanced at his watch, wondering how much longer until she would finish her meeting with her sisters to review insurance paperwork. Claire and Starr had driven down from Charleston to spend the day with her, which left him free to attend this benefit golf tournament *and* hang with his brothers. They were just finishing up the ninth hole, so he would be home before supper.

Sebastian clapped him on the back with a solid thud, the two of them the closest in height and build. "Are we going to play or are you going to laze around for the rest of the afternoon staring at your watch?"

The sun beat down unrelentingly on his head. Matthew shrugged his shoulders under his golf shirt, flexed his hand inside the leather glove, but still tension kinked through him. "Just gauging the course."

Jonah chuckled low, his attention only half with them as he watched some college-aged girl in a designer sun visor driving the course's drink cart around. "Yeah, right. We saw you say goodbye to your fiancée earlier," he said, no doubt referring to the kiss still scorching Matthew's veins. "What's up with her, dude? Why didn't you bring her by before? You wouldn't let us get away with that."

He hated lying to his family, but... Now he had this notion of letting things keep going as they were with Ashley. See where it led.

Keep enjoying what they did have.

Sebastian elbowed Jonah and pointed to the cluster of reporters gathering around the oceanside clubhouse in the distance. "Shut your trap. There's media everywhere."

Jonah pulled his gaze off the bleached blond coed in the drink cart with obvious reluctance and checked out the press gathering. "Yeah, right." He shoved a hand through his unruly curls in need of a hair cut. "Gotta keep up the good family name."

Kyle swished through practice swings with lanky grace. The workout fiend was always in motion, keeping in shape for his military career. "Damn, bro, thanks to you we can't do anything together anymore without it turning into a photo-op."

Matthew dropped a new ball on the ground. "I figured leaking this outing of ours would take some heat off Ashley for the day."

Kyle shaded his eyes against the harsh summer sun as he peered off in the direction of the press. "Giving them something else to talk about?"

"Pretty much." He swung... Watched... The ball landed on the green. "It's not like we haven't been dealing with this kind of coverage for most of our lives. I figured you could handle the heat."

Matthew climbed into his golf cart, Sebastian settling in beside him while their other brothers drove along behind. He guided the vehicle past rolling dunes with sea oats blowing in the muggy breeze.

Sebastian reached for his soda can in the holder as their clubs rattled in back. "So this woman's really gotten to you, then."

"I'm engaged to her." That in and of itself was a step he'd never expected to take again.

"Ah, come on. Be real around me, at least."

"Who says I'm not being real?" There had been more than a few moments with Ashley where he'd forgotten they were playing roles.

"You're actually going to marry her?" His brother peered over his Armani sunglasses.

"I didn't say that." Yeah, he was quibbling but this wasn't a conversation he was comfortable with. Not after a night that had jumbled all his carefully made plans. "I simply said we're engaged. She's a special, honest person who doesn't deserve how things went down."

"Bro, you are so toast." Sebastian shook his head, humor fading from his face as he replaced his drink in the holder. "Just be careful. Don't rush into anything until you're certain."

Hell. He should have seen where this was going given Sebastian's recent separation from his wife. They'd married too young, grown in different directions and it was tearing them both apart. Now that Matthew looked closer, he could see that his brother had lost weight in recent months, his angular face almost gaunt. He'd gone so long without a haircut, he would soon be sporting Jonah's length.

And he still wore his platinum wedding band.

Sebastian served as a great big reminder for how badly two well-meaning people could hurt each other in the end. Matthew hated that he couldn't do a damn thing to make this right for his younger brother.

He clapped his hand against Sebastian's shoulder. "I hear you and I'm sorry for the hell you're going through."

"I hear you, too, and I'm not trying to interfere, only adding my two cents from the hard knocks side of the romance world."

Matthew gripped the steering wheel as they whirred past a pelican perched on a wood pole. Damn it all, he'd been so caught up in his campaigning, he hadn't been there for his brother the way that he should have during what was undoubtedly the most painful time of his life. And how was that for a kick-in-the ass wake-up call about ill-advised marriages born of out-of-control emotions? "How much longer until the divorce is final?"

"This fall," Sebastian answered, his voice flat.

"A lot could happen between now and then." Look how quickly his life had been turned upside down.

"Too much already happened between now and then. We both simply want to move on without sacrificing any more blood in the process."

"I'm sorry, damn sorry. I really hoped you two could beat the odds."

"Me, too, bro. Me, too." Sebastian nudged his sunglasses firmly in place and looked away.

Message received loud and clear. Back off.

Silence stretched between them, broken only by the ever-present rustling of creatures in the underbrush that remained after the golf course had been hewn out of the wild area.

Finally, Sebastian's face spread into a smile, a little forced, but obviously where he wanted the tone to go. "Enough of this heart-and-guts bull. Let's get back to the game and I'll show you who's going to blow the odds to hell and back."

Matthew stopped the cart and retrieved a club from his leather bag in back. "I'm starting to think Mom has it right."

Kyle loped alongside them. "What do you mean?"

"The way she picked a friend to marry the second go round rather than signing on for all that rollercoaster emotional crap. Maybe we should all learn the lesson from her."

Jonah stopped short, a hank of curls falling over his forehead. "Are you flipping blind? Mom's absolutely crazy about the general."

"Yeah, yeah." Matthew waved aside his youngest brother's comment. "I know they're—God forgive me for saying this—hot for each other. Remember, I was there with you guys when we accidentally walked in on them in bed together."

Matthew shuddered right along with his brothers. What a day that had been catching their sainted mother *in flagrante delicto* with her longtime friend-turned-lover, a man she had since married.

Even their playboy brother Jonah looked rattled by just the mention of that brain-stunner of an event. "I really would have preferred to go through life believing we were all four immaculately conceived."

Sebastian made a referee T with his hands. "Okay, let's not go there again, even in our mind. But I think Jonah has a point," he continued in his naturally lawyerly logical tone, "Mom isn't just attracted to him, she really loves the general."

Matthew forced his ever-racing brain to slow and think back to his mom's Christmas wedding to Hank Renshaw. Sure the event had been romantically impulsive, but could there have been something more in his mother's eyes then? And now, as well? He thought of all the times her face lit up when her cell phone rang with the distinctive ringtone she'd programmed for only the general's calls.

Aside from successful, high-power political careers, his mom and her new husband shared a lot of views in common and didn't hesitate to take an hour from their busy schedules to sit on the porch swing and talk over glasses of wine.

Now that he looked at it from more of an analytical perspective, it seemed obvious. His mother and General Hank Renshaw were totally in love with each other.

How could he have been so self-delusional? Because he'd wanted reality to fit his need for low-key commitment—while still holding on to Ashley. Problem was, now he didn't have a solution to the mess he'd made of his and Ashley's lives. Although he did know one thing for certain.

No way in hell could he live without a repeat of what they'd shared the night before.

Back in the main house, Ashley stared out the guest bedroom window over the ocean, not too different a view than the one she'd grown up with at Aunt Libby's. Lordy, but she'd never needed the woman's support more than now when she faced the toughest decision of her life.

Even the ocean view and the soothing décor of the

guest room's delft-blue flowers accented with airy stripes did little to lower her stress level. Spending the afternoon with her foster sisters crunching the numbers and detailing the massive amount of work required to get Beachcombers up and running as a business again had been tougher than she'd expected. Once she rebuilt the place, it would be time to move on with her life—apart from Matthew. Even the thought of that hurt more than she'd expected.

However, continuing with this charade hurt, too. How long could she keep falling into bed—and tubs—with him without making a decision about their future one way or another?

Fantasizing about the man had been easy. Being with him was far more complicated and exciting. And scary. Why couldn't he have been a regular, everyday kind of guy, with a regular everyday sort of life?

She stared down at her engagement ring and practiced pulling it off her finger. Her hand felt so blasted bare. She clenched her fist to resist the urge to put the solitaire back in place and to hell with the consequences to her heart.

Ashley held the diamond up for the sun to glint off the facets. So many angles and nuances could be seen depending on which way she looked at the stone. And wasn't that much like her life? She had an important choice to make and her decision changed depending on which way she viewed the situation.

The air conditioner cranked on, swooshing a teasing gust over her neck almost as tantalizing as a lover's kiss. Then stronger, warmer.

She shivered, reflexively closing her fingers around the ring.

Matthew's lips pressed firmer against her skin. "Hello, beautiful."

She tried to force herself to relax as she turned in his arms. "I didn't hear you come in."

He skimmed his knuckles over her forehead. "You were certainly caught up thinking about something important. Did things go all right with your sisters?"

She blinked quickly as she shifted mental gears. God, she hadn't even been thinking about Beachcombers, which should totally have been her focus. "Everything went fine. There are lots of positives to focus on. The fire investigators tracked the problem to old wiring failing. Nothing we're liable for, so our insurance payment will come through smoothly. We can start contacting contractors right away."

He pressed a firm kiss to her mouth before hugging her. "That's great to hear. I'm glad for all three of you."

With his heartbeat under her ear and his musky scent all around her, the queen-size bed only five feet away seemed too enticing. "Let's go out to the living room. I know we're adults and all, but it doesn't seem right for your mother to find us in here together."

He winced. "Banish that thought here and now." Matthew backed a step but stroked her arms. "Don't worry, though. She just left, so you can relax."

"I can't do that." The ring seemed to gain weight in her grasp. "Relax, I mean."

He looked behind him and back again. "Are your sisters still here somewhere?"

"They left a half hour ago." She gathered up her words and let them roll free before she could stop herself. She unfurled her fingers, the engagement ring cupped in her palm. "Actually, I can't do this anymore."

Any hint of a smile faded from his face. "Do what precisely?"

Ashley raised her hand holding the solitaire, her hand already shaking at the thought of giving it back. Aside from her own reservations, she couldn't ignore fears of the opponent gaining momentum from her decision.

She would do her best to persuade Starr to step forward. Perhaps that would even encourage others who might have received the same treatment to open up.

Regardless, she couldn't be a party to perpetuating a lie, even as much as breaking things off with Matthew tore her apart inside. "Pretend to be engaged. Lying to the press has been difficult enough. Lying to my *sisters* this afternoon was hell. They probably already suspect anyway."

"Well, as a matter of fact—" he clasped both of her hands in his "—I was thinking about that myself while golfing with my brothers."

Her stomach twisted. So this was it. They would break things off and she would be back in Charleston with real memories to replace the fantasies. Except reality had been so much more amazing than any make-believe. "And your thoughts led you to what conclusion?"

His grip tightened on her arms. "What do you say we give it a try for real? No more pretending."

She couldn't have heard what she thought. Her stomach clenched tighter than his hold on her. "I think you're going to need to repeat that because I'm certain I couldn't have heard you correctly."

He lifted her left hand and thumbed the bare spot. "Let's keep the ring in place and get to know each other better, hang out—"

"Have sex?"

"I sure as hell hope so."

Matthew's resurrected grin left her in no doubt of how much he wanted her. Except she needed more than that now. She deserved more. "While you were golfing with your brothers, you decided we need to hang out more and have sex?"

"I'm not expressing myself well, which is damned odd considering I'm used to crafting the right sound bite—which should tell you something about how you screw with my head." His smile went from charming to wicked in a flash of perfect teeth. "How about I try this again. Let's get to know each other better, build a, uh…" He gestured for the word, his gaze scanning the boat-speckled horizon as if answers bobbed on the gleaming waters.

"Relationship. The word is *relationship,* Matthew." It was tough for her to consider, too, but at least she could say the word without becoming tongue-tied.

"Yeah, right. That." He skimmed a finger along his collar, which would have been understandable if he hadn't been wearing a freaking Polo shirt with the top two buttons undone.

"Sounds to me like you're describing sex buddies and sex buddies don't exchange rings." How odd that a few weeks ago, sex buddies would have actually sounded like a fun fantasy come true. Except now this ring screwed up everything because it taunted her with the deeper sentiments that she wanted—deserved—from life someday.

"What do you expect from me?" Matthew stared down at her, frustration sparking in his gem-green eyes. "Do you want me to say I love you? I've been in love before and it takes a while. I haven't known you long enough to be sure about something like that. But I can say that I think I could love you someday. So why break things off when there's that possibility out there?"

Could love her *someday?* Talk about a rousing endorsement.

Then her mind hitched on one phrase to the exclusion of everything else he'd said. "You've been in love before?"

He went stone still.

"Matthew? Who was it?" She couldn't resist asking, too darn curious about the woman who had managed to steal his heart. "The press has linked you to plenty of women over the years and certainly speculated about more than a few of them recently, but nothing serious ever seemed to come of those liaisons. I think that's part of the reason they've gone so snap happy over our fake engagement."

"You're probably correct," he conceded, although still neatly dodging her question.

Her curiosity only heightened. She wasn't sure why it should matter so much when she was determined to break things off. She should be running for the door before her will faltered.

Still, she had to ask. "Then who is the woman? I think even my pretend-fiancée status gives me the right to ask."

He started to reach for his collar again before dropping his arm to his side as he stepped around her to peer out the window. "Someone I knew in college—Dana." He stuffed his fists into his pockets, his jaw hard. "Dana and I became engaged unexpectedly fast and before I could introduce her to the family, she died."

Her heart squeezed inside her chest with sympathy, and an impending sense of how he'd never been hers from the beginning.

"I'm so sorry." She tentatively touched his shoulder, unable to resist offering comfort for those long-ago hurts. She knew well from her parents' abandonment how long those emotional aches could persist. "It must have been horrible to lose her."

"It was," he said simply, but the two words carried more pain than any lengthy monologue could have. His muscles tensed under her touch.

"What happened?" she asked gently.

"She—Dana—had a heart defect, something rare that had gone undetected." He scrubbed his hand over his face, his jaw flexing. Pain pulsed from him as palpably as if he'd shouted the words.

"You really loved Dana." Part of her ached to comfort him. Another part, a new stronger piece of herself asserted she deserved that same intense love. She couldn't accept being a second-best sex buddy.

Ashley stepped away from Matthew. She carefully placed her fairy-tale diamond and all the precious multi-faceted dreams it had held on to the bedside table. "I'm sorry, Matthew, this is just how it has to end—"

The phone jangled by her engagement ring, jolting her back a step.

Matthew hesitated, his eyes holding hers while the ringing continued. She waved him toward the call. She should call her sisters for a ride. They shouldn't be too far away since they'd dropped her off less than an hour ago.

His eyes still narrowed and locked on her, he crossed to pick up the receiver. "Landis residence."

She started to reach for her cell when something fierce in Matthew's expression as he took the call made her hesitate.

No more than four thudding heartbeats later, he scowled and reached for the television remote resting beside the lamp. "Right, got it, Brent. I'm tuning in now."

He thumbed the remote, activating the flat-screen television mounted on the wall. What could the press have come up with on them this time? Pictures of them would be embarrassing but useless. Still she could see from Matthew's frown this wasn't happy news.

The TV screen blazed to life with a newsflash that was already in progress. A photo-inset box appeared in the upper right-hand corner behind the newscaster's head, complete with a picture of Matthew at the golf course...

With his arm around a blond hottie plastered to his side.

Ten

"So do we shoot him outright or do we torture him first?" Her expression fierce, Starr leaned her elbows on her restaurant table across from Ashley and Claire.

Ashley tried to shake free the numbed sensation still dogging her even two hours after the call from Matthew's campaign manager. There had barely been time for Matthew to turn to Ashley and state, "The photos aren't what you think," before his family had begun pouring into the house for a troubleshooting session.

Sure he'd had an explanation about the water girl

at the golf course throwing herself at him, which left him instinctively steadying her at an inopportune time since the press packed the parking lot. His brothers affirmed he didn't know her—although unlucky for Matthew, his brothers had been in search of food at that particular moment.

He'd been so busy trying to convince her, yet the whole water-girl incident felt like nothing to her in comparison to his revelation about Dana. Ashley believed there was nothing to those golf-course photos.

Her problem boiled down to trust on a larger scale. The need to trust he could ever have deep feelings for another woman again. The belief that he could someday fall for *her*.

Her sisters had called almost immediately and turned around to come back to Hilton Head. Claire had told her—in a tone that brooked no argument—that they were on their way. Ashley had been more than grateful for the opportunity to escape the mayhem of campaign central working damage control.

Which was how she ended up in a dark back corner of an out-of-the-way seafood restaurant, wearing sunglasses and a ball cap.

Ashley scratched under the hat. She didn't want her life "spun" anymore.

Starr dragged the bread basket over from the middle of the table, the pregnant woman's appetite apparently insatiable. "So? Quick death or torture?"

Claire unfolded and refolded her napkin precisely. "To think, the press missed the real story when they actually bought into that engagement story hook, line and sinker."

Ashley snatched the perfectly creased napkin from her sister's hands. "Who says it isn't real? I never gave you any indication otherwise."

"Oh come on, we know you." Claire patted Ashley's hand, still bare of the engagement ring. "You're too much like me. You wouldn't get engaged to someone you didn't know well."

"You've never done anything impulsive in the romance department?" She waited to see how her sister would dodge that question since they all knew Claire had gotten pregnant in a one-night stand with a friend who was now her head-over-heels-in-love husband and father to their beautiful baby girl.

Claire raised a perfectly arched blond eyebrow. "Somebody's not playing nice today." She reached to the empty table next to them and snagged a new napkin. "But you're forgiven because of the stress."

Ashley struggled to shrug off the defensiveness. These were her sisters. She couldn't lie to them anymore. Perhaps it was time she also stopped lying to herself.

She rubbed the bare spot where the engagement ring had rested. "It doesn't matter now anyway. Matthew and I are over."

Or rather Matthew had been trying to bring up the possibility of staying together and she'd cut him off short.

Claire studied her with a gentle concern reminiscent of Aunt Libby's maternal care. "Is this about the suggestive photos?"

"The ones of me and him, or the ones of her and him?" Ashley crinkled her nose. "The one of him at the golf course actually doesn't worry me beyond what damage it could do to his campaign. I'm certain the picture was a setup."

And oddly enough, she was sure. She trusted him with physical faithfulness. Totally. He'd never been anything but honest with her, even when it hurt. She'd heard clearly enough in his voice how much he'd loved that woman from long ago, a real romance that concerned her far more than any manufactured one on the evening news.

Starr sagged back in her seat, tearing into another piece of bread while the other guests and televisions buzzed loudly enough to afford them privacy to talk.

"I guess this means we don't get to enjoy torturing your hunky senatorial candidate."

Ashley allowed herself a half smile. "I would appreciate it if you took a pass on that this go-round."

Claire patted her hand, her nail tapping the spot where the ring used to nestle waiting for a wedding band to complete the set. "Now your schedule is free and clear again."

Ashley tugged the sunglasses off. To hell with anonymity. She wanted to see life clearly now more than ever. "Don't worry, I will uphold my end of the obligations with reopening Beachcombers."

Claire and Starr exchanged a loaded look before Claire tugged a folder from her overlarge purse. "We were actually getting ready to turn around and come back when the news story broke."

"Turn around? Why?" When they still hesitated so long a waitress managed to work her way past with a steaming platter of crab legs, Ashley pressed harder, "Please, don't hold anything back. I've been up-front with you and I'm going to be hurt if you aren't equally open with me."

Claire twisted her napkin in a totally un-Claire disregard for order, which relayed just how nervous she must be. "We weren't lying about anything earlier. We simply omitted some thoughts we've been having about the whole rebuilding process."

Starr shoved away the now nearly empty bread basket. "What do you plan to do with your future, after the election—if you and Matthew don't stay together?"

"I imagined we'll be busy renovating Beach-combers." The possibility of taking him up on his offer still felt so alien she hadn't thought that far ahead. She needed to get her head together and in the present. She looked from sister to sister. "What are you both keeping from me? Was there something wrong with the insurance adjustment after all?"

"No, nothing like that," Claire rushed to reassure her.

Ashley relaxed back in her chair. "Okay, then. I appreciate all the times you helped me and protected me and built me up over the years." She injected strength in her words to match the steel in her spine. "But I'm not that shy, insecure little kid anymore. Could you please stop treating me like a child and welcome me into your grown-ups club?"

Starr covered Ashley's hand with hers. "We love you. It's hard not to worry."

"Thank you." She squeezed Starr's hand and reached for Claire's, as well. "I love you both, too. So tell me. What's with all the secret looks? Come on, Claire? Spill it."

"We're just wondering if we should look into options other than reopening Beachcombers."

Claire's words hovered over the table between them, heavy and unexpected.

Ashley finally got her brain off stun long enough to speak. "You mean level Aunt Libby's house?"

"No, not that." Starr waved aside that possibility, thank God. "We could use the insurance money to restore the place to its former glory. Then sell it. Let a family live and grow and flourish there."

Claire angled forward. "We could split the proceeds three ways and it will still give us each the chance to pursue any career dreams we want. I can open my own catering business with more flexible hours for the baby."

Ashley turned to Starr. "And you feel the same way about this?"

"Yes, sweetie. I do. I've always wanted to go back to art school and study abroad. Sure, my husband can afford it, but I appreciate the chance to finance it myself. You have your degree and this would give you a nice financial cushion. But we don't want you to feel like you don't have a home."

Their plan made sense. They both had husbands, homes, children and unique career dreams of their own. And she had…

A wonderfully unconventional family who loved her and a quirky old lady who'd taught her to value herself. None of that would change because of owning or selling a particular house.

Ashley squeezed her sisters' hands. "We have a bond, the three of us, that goes beyond any house. The memories Aunt Libby gave us are a far stronger link than any home could ever be. And I think she would like the notion of a family being brought up in her home."

Across the restaurant, one of the patrons reached to turn up the volume on one of the televisions. Starr's eyes widening gave her the first hint that she'd better check it out.

Ashley pivoted in her chair for a better view of the screen. A local news announcement had interrupted the sporting event. "Senatorial candidate Matthew Landis's campaign has just announced he will be making a statement to the press outside his headquarters."

What could he be planning to say? She'd left the family gathering before a consensus had been reached. No doubt if they didn't act soon, his opponent would beat him to the punch and no telling what he would concoct. Damn shame nobody ever seemed interested in posting compromising photos of Martin Stewart. But then Matthew was the forerunner right now, so tearing him down made for better news and a tighter race—which generated more public interest.

Where did she fit into all of this?

She looked at her sisters and thought of how even logical Claire had begun following her heart. Ashley stared at the pictures of Matthew on the television screen—one of him with her, then the one from the golf course, followed by an image of him alone.

From the moment she'd seen that image of him with the blonde, she'd known he wasn't seeing anyone else. Aside from the fact he'd been with her nearly every second of every day, she knew him to be an honorable man. He'd even been willing to put his campaign, his life's dream, in jeopardy to make things right for her.

How come she'd been so comfortable trusting him, but unable to trust in herself? She wanted to be a part of his life. He'd told her he wanted to be a part of hers and then shared something intensely personal and painful about his past. That indicated a willingness to take things to a deeper level than before and she should be brave enough to explore the possibility.

Life wasn't going to get less complicated if she walked away from him. In fact, already her heart was telling her turning her back on the feelings developing between them would lead to complications that would hurt her for the rest of her life.

He'd supported her through a scandal that was

every bit as much her own fault as his. He deserved her support now. She was ready to fight for her place in the forefront of Matthew Landis's life.

Ashley pushed back her chair and stood, gathering her purse. "My dear sisters, I agree. Renovate and sell Beachcombers. It's time, time for a lot of things." She gathered her purse and her resolve. "I'm going to Matthew's press conference to be with him."

Where she now knew she belonged, beside the man she loved.

Matthew stood in the foyer of his campaign headquarters, gathering his thoughts. In less than ninety seconds, he would step outside and address the media about his plummeting poll numbers.

His staff stayed in the main office, their conversations a controlled low buzz as they gave him the space he needed to collect himself before stepping outside. He blocked out the noise from television monitors and kept his eyes off all the posters packing the walls.

He had speech notes tucked in his pocket, words that could end his political career, but unavoidable. He had to stop this press war that was tearing Ashley apart, and if that meant he lost the election then so be it. A man had to make a stand for what mattered most.

He hadn't been able to do anything for Dana, but

he damn well could fall on his sword for Ashley. He couldn't live with himself if he ruined her life to save a career.

In losing Ashley, he'd blown the biggest opportunity of his life, way bigger than any senate seat.

He would find another way to change the freaking world. He had the resources and the drive. Ashley had shown him there were other effective approaches to life than just his bullheaded full speed ahead manner.

Matthew checked his watch again. Thirty seconds. He reached for the knob to step out and join Brent on the porch.

A hand fell on his shoulder. Matthew jolted. Damn. He'd been so preoccupied he hadn't even heard anyone approach.

He pivoted to find... "Ashley? What are you doing here?"

Her brown eyes gleamed with a wide intensity, totally focused on him in a way that lured him, distracted him, at the worst possible moment.

"I came in through the back. Your mother met me and let me in." She gripped his lapels, energy pulsing from her, her long hair rising in a staticky halo around her. "Matthew, what are you planning to say to those reporters?"

"The truth. That I've let them dictate my decisions in a way that has hurt others. That if I'm going to be an effective senator for my constituents, I have to be willing to take the flack that might come my way from the press." He resisted the urge to gather her against him even as he ached to skim his hands along her sweet curves under her lemon-yellow sundress. "I'm going to say whatever it takes to protect you *and* set you free."

She slipped her hand through the crook of his arm. "I'm going with you."

"Like hell." He scowled.

She scowled right back. "Just try and stop me."

Before he could blink, she'd ducked under his other arm and slipped out the front door, straight toward the press conference. Hell, she was determined. And hot.

And headed for trouble.

He bolted after her, almost slamming into Brent, who was attempting to hide the panicked look on his face that appeared whenever things weren't following his perfectly scripted agenda. The instant spent working his way around his campaign manager cost Matthew the precious time needed to catch Ashley before she took her place in front of the podium.

Complete with a microphone and a captive media audience.

"Good afternoon, ladies and gentlemen of the press. I know you expected to hear from Congressman

Landis today, but I have to confess to being a bit pushy in wanting to get my two cents in first for the record."

She flashed the gentle smile of hers combined with her shy way of glancing through her lashes at the crowd. How odd that he'd never before noticed her ramrod straight steely spine under that gorgeous mass of red hair. Those years in a back brace had honed strength in her nobody was going to cow, not even the most sharklike members of the media.

"I imagine we've gathered to talk about revealing photos."

Her bluntness stunned everyone still. For all of three heartbeats and then photographers started snapping away again.

"Oh, but wait, we already discussed those pictures of me."

A giggle started in the back, slowly working its way to the front until everyone relaxed and joined in. Interesting how everyone seemed to be perspiring from the summer heat—except for cool, collected Ashley.

"I appreciate that you're all here. You offer a valuable service in getting the message out. Today, I simply want to make sure the message is factually correct so we're not wasting time with messy legalities later."

Whoa, she had the spine set on mega-strong today.

Brent shook his head slowly. "My God, she's got the press eating out of the palm of her hand. I've never seen anything like her."

Matthew turned back to stare at Ashley bathed in the beauty of her glowing self-confidence that radiated stronger than even the South Carolina sun. "Me, either."

Ashley nodded to the crowd from the podium. "Now, I happen to believe that a photo of a popular candidate, in his golf clothes, on the golf course, standing by a golf-course employee isn't particularly scandal worthy. But that's easier for me to say because I know Matthew and I trust him. I realize that trust takes time."

He didn't doubt the surety in her words and wondered why he'd ever thought she couldn't handle whatever life threw at her. Ashley was a helluva lot stronger than he'd ever given her credit for.

She was absolutely incredible.

Her tone shifted subtly from congenial to factual. "That's what a campaign is all about, taking the time to get to know the candidate. Learning to trust him to see to our best interests in the senate. I, for one, would like to hear more about Matthew's strategy for guiding our country rather than about photos that divert your attention from getting to know the smart, dynamic leadership style of Matthew Landis."

Listening to her talk, Matthew felt a kick in his gut he'd never expected to experience again, one far stronger than anything he remembered experiencing before but recognized all the same. *He loved this woman.*

She glanced his way with a steady smile that sent a fresh surge of emotion through him. "If you're ready to speak now, Matthew, I would especially like to hear more about your innovative plans to sponsor legislation targeted at helping to strengthen benefits in our foster-care system."

He wanted to talk to Ashley, tell her he loved her and yeah, he wanted her, too, but it was definitely about more than being sex buddies. However, the things he had to say to her were private and the sooner he dispensed with the press, the sooner he could get Ashley all to himself.

Matthew collected his thoughts and stepped toward the microphone. He could present that particular talking point of Ashley's proposed speech blindfolded with his hands behind his back. And after he finished the press conference, he had an entirely different discussion in mind. Except the dialogue with Ashley wouldn't be as easy to deliver and the outcome odds were shaky at best.

But he wouldn't let the opportunity of a lifetime pass him by.

* * *

Ashley applauded the end of Matthew's speech with a mix of pride and trepidation. While they'd averted a campaign catastrophe today, would she be able to turn things around for them after she'd all but pitched his ring in his face earlier?

If she trusted the look in his eyes when he smiled at her, then they weren't anywhere near over. Lucky for her, she'd learned to trust him—and more importantly, she'd learned to trust in herself.

Brent ducked his head close to her ear. "You took a real risk out there, Ashley."

"He's worth it." She soaked in the broad set of Matthew's shoulders, the honest connection in his eyes when he spoke with individual voters.

Brent extended his hand. "I'm sorry for underestimating you. I should be a better judge of character than that by now."

"Apology accepted." She clasped his palm and shook firmly. "You were only looking out for Matthew, which I appreciate."

Matthew waved farewell to the crowd and joined her, leading her and Brent back inside headquarters where the televisions already blared with reports of the media conference. "Hey, Brent, get your own lady. This one's taken."

Ashley elbowed Matthew in the side. "Did you ever consider you're the one who's taken?"

"Good point." Matthew scooped her into his arms as he'd done a week ago when he'd saved her life.

She may have squeaked in surprise, but she didn't even bother protesting and simply settled in for the ride while his campaign staff cheered them on. How far she and Matthew had come in just a week since he'd carried her from the flaming Beachcombers.

He stepped into his office and kicked the door closed. Keeping her arms around his neck, she slid her feet to the floor, leaning into him, urging his face down to meet hers. How could she have ever thought she would be able to turn her back on this, on him?

Matthew nuzzled her ear. "You were…"

"Amazing?" She angled back to grin up at him.

"Absolutely," he confirmed without hesitation. "I can't believe I was worried about protecting you from the press. I should have turned you loose on them right from the start."

She wouldn't have credited herself with the ability to field them that first day when they'd captured revealing pictures of her. But the past week spent learning about herself, learning about real love, she'd discovered there were things out there far more important than worrying what others thought of her. "I'm just glad to have been of help. I believe in you and your message."

"Thank you. That means more to me than I think you realize. I'm sorry about the way we left things earlier." He clasped both of her hands in his. "I want to talk to you about Dana."

"It's okay." She brushed her fingers over his mouth. "I understand."

"I need to say this." He clasped her wrist and lowered her hand. "I should have said it the right way earlier, but I don't have much practice speaking about the past. In fact, I don't have any experience with it at all."

"You haven't told *anyone* about Dana?"

He certainly hadn't mentioned that earlier and the admission touched her heart in a new and unexpected way. He'd chosen her over anyone else when it came to sharing such an important part of his past. What a time to realize that Matthew *had* put her first, even before his own relatives.

"Since my family hadn't met her and she didn't have any family to meet me, nobody knew how serious things had gotten. Nobody until you, now."

No way could she miss the importance of him sharing this with her and how that linked them. "Thank you for choosing me to be the one you told."

She only wished she'd been less defensive earlier when he'd tried to discuss it with her.

He cupped her face in his hands, his green eyes glinting with intensity. "I want you to understand that the past doesn't, in any way, detract from what I feel for you." He tapped her lips, paused to stroke a slow, sensual circle. "And just to clarify in case there's any doubt about how I feel for you, I love you, Ashley Carson. I. Love. You."

The magic words. Even in her fantasies she hadn't dared go there, but then perhaps that was good. Reality definitely beat any dream relationship in a landslide victory. "I know you do, but it's still awesome to hear you say it." She nipped his thumb. "And quite convenient since I happen to love you, too."

His ragged sigh shared just how much her words meant to him, a strong man so determined to take on the world full speed ahead.

Matthew slipped his hand into his pocket and pulled it back out to reveal... Her engagement ring rested in his palm. "I'll understand if you would rather have a different one to mark our new beginning, but either way, I want our engagement to be real this time."

She placed her hand over his, over the diamond and the real promise it now held. "This is exactly the one I want. I wouldn't change a thing about our past because it brought us to this perfect moment. Yes, I'll marry you."

He pressed a hard, quick kiss to her lips before pulling back with a smile. "I'm not going to give you time to change your mind, you know."

Matthew slid the solitaire back in place.

She closed her fist, locking the ring on tight. "Nobody's going to pry it off my hand again."

"You're a mighty force to be reckoned with."

And she'd only just begun finding her footing.

Ashley looped her arms around his neck, arching up on her toes for another kiss she knew would lead her to the perfect end to a perfect day. "I'm more than ready to make this relationship real."

Epilogue

November: Election Night

"Latest polling reports are in," the widescreen plasma television blared in the family great room at the Landis compound.

Ashley held her breath as the second before the announcement seemed to stretch out with a slow-motion quality. Sitting with Matthew on the sofa, she gripped his hand, their family and friends around them. Five months ago, she never could have imagined how her life would change because of one impulsive decision to take a risk with the man of her dreams.

But here she was after months of campaigning, totally loving Matthew and finding she also fully enjoyed the new world he'd opened for her.

She'd once thought herself a background, live-in-the-shadows kind of person. Now she'd discovered the rush of being at the epicenter of reaching out to others. And when she needed to recharge? She had an even larger new family to embrace, a family who'd all come to share in this moment.

Her sisters and their husbands blended right in with the Landis brothers and General Renshaw's adult children. The general and Ginger had been an unexpected blessing in her life, taking her on as one of their own. Nobody could replace Aunt Libby, but Lordy, it felt good to experience the warmth and acceptance of parental love again.

Ashley squeezed Matthew's strong hand as the television announcer continued, "With ninety-one percent of the precincts reporting, the numbers indicate a clear victory for…"

She forced herself to breathe, keep her focus on Matthew and the TV rather than the hubbub behind them from the small media crew that had been allowed into the Landis compound to report about this moment.

"…the new senator from South Carolina, Matthew Landis," the announcer concluded.

The already crowded room overflowed with cheers. Matthew gathered Ashley into a tight hug. As much as she wanted to stay right there and revel, she knew there were others in the room who deserved to celebrate with him.

She kissed him quickly, intensely, before pulling back. "Congratulations, Senator Landis."

He nuzzled her ear, the gentle rasp of his whiskers sending a shiver of excitement mingling with the surge of joy. "Thank you, Mrs. Landis."

And what an added rush to hear her new name.

They'd quietly eloped two weeks ago, unable to wait any longer to make it official. While the immediate family already knew, she and Matthew would tell the rest of the world during his acceptance speech. They hadn't wanted their marriage to be tied up with the election outcome. The vows they'd spoken were all about them and not any political agenda.

After a final searing kiss, they eased apart and the rest of their huge wonderful family surrounded them in hugs and congrats. Ashley leaned into his muscular side since Matthew seemed determined to keep his arm around her waist.

Cameras continued to flash while streamers unfurled in the air. Hats, bunting and posters instantly redecorated the house with Senator Landis paraphernalia. A champagne bottle popped some-where in the distance, and thankfully Ginger seemed to have the first interview well in hand so Matthew could enjoy more celebratory time with the family.

Kyle clapped him on the shoulder. "Don't be getting the big head now, brother. I can still whoop your butt in golf any day."

"Of course you can." Matthew grinned good-naturedly. "Golfing is like a college degree for you Air Force guys."

Laughing and nodding along in agreement, Jonah passed Sebastian folded cash.

Matthew slugged his youngest brother in the arm, laughing. "Jonah, bro, you bet against me?"

Jonah slugged right back. "Dude, we were only betting on the spread of your landslide."

Ashley patted her brother-in-law's cheek. "You're forgiven then."

Matthew toyed with Ashley's ponytail streaming down her back from the gold clasp. "So tell me then, guys, who bet for the largest win?"

Sebastian—the most reserved of the group—offered up one of his rare smiles as he pocketed the cash. "We'll carry that secret to our grave."

Ashley basked in the moment as the general and Ginger beamed with parental pride. It didn't even bother her that the small hand-picked media group in the back recorded each embrace and high five and hug. She had nothing to hide and total confidence in the love she and Matthew had found.

As the media's attention swapped from Ginger to the general for a comment, Ashley turned to Matthew. "When will we be heading to campaign headquarters to give your acceptance speech?"

"Soon enough." He skimmed his lips over her temple, the warm scent of his aftershave teasing her senses. "First, I want to have a minute alone with you before we leave."

She flattened her hand to his chest, the cotton of his button-down shirt offering a tormenting barrier to the muscles beneath. "I think everyone would understand us stealing a moment to freshen up."

Matthew took her hand and led her through the throng with amazing speed. As they made their way toward the hall, her sisters each gave her another quick hug before exchanging secretive looks. Ashley started to quiz them, then Matthew distracted her with another kiss and before she knew it they were inside the bedroom she'd used when first staying in this home.

He kicked the door closed behind them, gathering her to his chest and sealing his mouth to hers for the kind of tongue-tangling, soul-searching kisses they wouldn't have dared exchange in front of any camera.

Matthew eased away only to rest his forehead on

hers. "I want to thank you for making all of this possible."

"You would have won with or without me." She cupped his handsome face in her hands.

"Since I've had enough of debates for a while, I'm not going to argue your point." He turned his head to press a lingering kiss in each of her palms. "But I want you to understand how much more this moment means because you're in my life, how much more connected I feel to what I'll be doing because of the insights you've given me."

His compliment touched her as deeply as any intimate caress they'd exchanged. "That's a lovely thing to say. Thank you."

"I want to give you something in return."

"You already have." This whole experience had helped her mine for depths inside herself she'd never known she possessed. "I have you, our family, our future."

"But I want you to have a home."

"Home will be where we're together."

"While I agree with you on that one, I also know how much you're giving up by splitting our lives between D.C. and here." He reached to the end table and picked up a folder she hadn't even noticed when they'd entered.

Probably because whenever he touched her she didn't notice much of anything else.

Matthew passed her an official-looking document.

Ashley frowned, studying the crisp paper in her hand, her mind scrambling to make sense of the words she saw but couldn't bring herself to comprehend, to believe. "This is the deed to Beachcombers, to Aunt Libby's mansion."

"Yes it is," he answered with a smug smile.

"But it already sold." An event she had accepted even though a piece of her heart still ached over that farewell. Except now that she stared at the name on the deed… No wonder her foster sisters had exchanged that knowing look a few moments ago.

"It sold to you. Sebastian took care of the purchasing process so as to mask my name from any of the transactions, and then I transferred the title to you." He thumbed a tear from her cheek she hadn't even known she'd shed. "We'll obviously spend a large portion of time in D.C., but we have to keep an official residence in South Carolina. So I thought we could make Aunt Libby's house in Charleston our official South Carolina residence."

She clasped the deed to her heart. "Are you sure? What about your family home here?"

"Absolutely sure." His green eyes glinted with unmistakable certainty. "Charleston is plenty close enough to Hilton Head for family visits. And you'll be near your sisters. The carriage house here will be too small once we start having kids."

Children. Hers and Matthew's. "I like the sound of that very much. Thank you. Those two simple words don't seem like enough, but there aren't words for how much this means to me."

Already she could envision all the ways she would want to shape the place into a home for them. Basic repairs had been completed and she wanted to stay true to the original décor of the traditional Southern mansion. But also with central AC, a state-of-the-art kitchen and adjoining rooms for her sisters to visit with their families.

Noise floated from the floor below, reminding her their alone time would be short tonight. A doorbell rang, no doubt more staff stopping by to congratulate the new senator. Fireworks popped in the distance, dogs barked in response. A light strobed right through the shades on the window as another news van pulled up outside.

Yet Matthew never once looked away from her face, his whole attention totally focused on her. "I'm glad you're happy about this. I want us to have our own place. The family compound idea worked well for a bachelor blowing in and out of town, but you and I deserve some privacy to explore the vast benefits of married life." His eyes took on an altogether different gleam, decidedly wicked.

"You're totally not a bachelor anymore." She relaxed into the arms of the man who'd stolen her heart and given her his own in return.

He raised her ring finger to his mouth and kissed the spot where her engagement ring and wedding band rested side by side. "Lucky for me, I went for the win."

* * * * *

*Don't miss the next Landis brother story,
when we get to learn all about
Sebastian and his soon-to-be-ex,
available in September from Silhouette Desire.*

*The editors at Harlequin Blaze have
never been afraid to push the limits—
tempting readers with the forbidden,
whetting their appetites with a
wide variety of story lines.
But now we're breaking the
final barrier—the time barrier.*

*In July, watch for BOUND TO PLEASE
by fan favorite Hope Tarr,
Harlequin Blaze's first ever
historical romance—a story that's truly
Blaze-worthy in every sense.*

Here's a sneak peek...

Brianna stretched out beside Ewan, languid as a cat, and promptly fell asleep. Midday sunshine streamed into the chamber, bathing her lovely, long-limbed body in golden light, the sea-scented breeze wafting inside to dry the damp red-gold tendrils curling about her flushed face. Propping himself up on one elbow, Ewan slid his gaze over her. She looked beautiful and whole, satisfied and sated, and altogether happier than he had so far seen her. A slight smile curved her beautiful lips as though she must be in the midst of a lovely dream. She'd molded her lush, lovely body to his and laid her head in the curve of his shoulder and settled in to sleep beside him. For the longest while he lay there turned toward her, content to watch her sleep, at near perfect peace.

Not wholly perfect, for she had yet to answer

his marriage proposal. Still, she wanted to make a baby with him, and Ewan no longer viewed her plan as the travesty he once had. He wanted children—sons to carry on after him, though a bonny little daughter with flame-colored hair would be nice, too. But he also wanted more than to simply plant his seed and be on his way. He wanted to lie beside Brianna night upon night as she increased, rub soothing unguents into the swell of her belly, knead the ache from her back and make slow, gentle love to her. He wanted to hold his newly born child in his arms and look down into Brianna's tired but radiant face and blot the perspiration from her brow and be a husband to her in every way.

He gave her a gentle nudge. "Brie?"

"Hmm?"

She rolled onto her side and he captured her against his chest. One arm wrapped about her waist, he bent to her ear and asked, "Do you think we might have just made a baby?"

Her eyes remained closed, but he felt her tense against him. "I don't know. We'll have to wait and see."

He stroked his hand over the flat plane of her belly. "You're so small and tight it's hard to imagine you increasing."

"All women increase no matter how large or small they start out. I may not grow big as a croft, but I'll be big enough, though I have hopes I may not waddle like a duck, at least not too badly."

The reference to his fair-day teasing was not lost on him. He grinned. "Brianna MacLeod grown so large she must sit still for once in her life. I'll need the proof of my own eyes to believe it."

Despite their banter, he felt his spirits dip. Assuming they were so blessed, he wouldn't have the chance to see her thus. By then he would be long gone, restored to his clan according to the sad bargain they'd struck. He opened his mouth to ask her to marry him again and then clamped it closed, not wanting to spoil the moment, but the unspoken words weighed like a millstone on his heart.

The damnable bargain they'd struck was proving to be a devil's pact indeed.

* * * * *

Will these two star-crossed lovers
find their sexily-ever-after?
Find out in BOUND TO PLEASE
by Hope Tarr,
available in July wherever
Harlequin® Blaze™ books are sold.

HIGH-SOCIETY SECRET PREGNANCY

Park Avenue Scandals

Self-made millionaire Max Rolland had given
up on love until he meets socialite fundraiser
Julia Prentice. After their encounter Julia finds
herself pregnant, but a mysterious blackmailer
threatens to use this surprise pregnancy and ruin
his reputation. Max must decide whether to turn
his back on the woman carrying his child or risk
everything, including his heart....

**Don't miss the next installment of
the Park Avenue Scandals series—
Front Page Engagement
by Laura Wright—
coming in August 2008
from Silhouette Desire!**

Always Powerful, Passionate and Provocative.

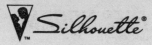

Silhouette®

Romantic
SUSPENSE

**Sparked by Danger,
Fueled by Passion.**

Conard County: The Next Generation

When he learns the truth about his father, military
man Ethan Parish is determined to reunite with his
long-lost family in Wyoming. On his way into town,
he clashes with policewoman Connie Halloran,
whose captivating beauty entices him. When
Connie's daughter is threatened, Ethan must use
his military skills to keep her safe. Together they
race against time to find the little girl and confront
the dangers inherent in family secrets.

Look for

*A Soldier's
Homecoming*

by *New York Times*
bestselling author
Rachel Lee

Available in July wherever you buy books.

REQUEST YOUR FREE BOOKS!

2 FREE NOVELS PLUS 2 FREE GIFTS!

Silhouette Desire®

Passionate, Powerful, Provocative!

SDES08R

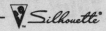

SPECIAL EDITION™

Little did hotel-chain CFO Tom Holloway
realize that his new executive assistant
spelled trouble. But even though
single mom Shelly Winston was planted
by Holloway's worst enemy to take him
down, Shelly was no dupe—she had
a mind of her own and an eye for
her handsome boss.

Look for

IN BED
WITH THE BOSS

by *USA TODAY* bestselling author
CHRISTINE RIMMER

*Available July
wherever you buy books.*

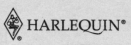

COMING NEXT MONTH

#1879 HIGH-SOCIETY SECRET PREGNANCY—
Maureen Child
Park Avenue Scandals
With her shocking pregnancy about to be leaked to the press, she has no choice but to marry the millionaire with whom she spent one passionate night.

#1880 DANTE'S WEDDING DECEPTION—Day Leclaire
The Dante Legacy
He'd lied and said he was her loving husband. For this Dante bachelor had to discover the truth behind the woman claiming to have lost her memory.

#1881 BOUND BY THE KINCAID BABY—Emilie Rose
The Payback Affairs
A will and an orphaned infant had brought them together. Now they had to decide if passion would tear them apart.

#1882 BILLIONAIRE'S FAVORITE FANTASY—Jan Colley
She'd unknowingly slept with her boss! And now the billionaire businessman had no intention of letting her get away.

#1883 THE CEO TAKES A WIFE—Maxine Sullivan
With only twelve months to produce an heir it was imperative he find the perfect bride...no matter what the consequences!

#1884 THE DESERT LORD'S BRIDE—Olivia Gates
Throne of Judar
The marriage had been arranged. And their attraction, unexpected. But would the heir to the throne choose the crown over the woman in his bed?